MAGIC, MYSTERY & MURDER

2ND THURSDAY WRITERS SHORT STORY
ANTHOLOGY

EDITORS: CORNELIA FEYE

TAMARA MERRILL

KONSTELLATION
PRESS

This book is a work of fiction. Names, characters, businesses, organizations, places, events, and incidents are either product of the author's imagination or are used fictitiously. Any resemblance to actual persons, living or dead, events, or locales is entirely coincidental.

Published by Konstellation Press, San Diego, CA, USA

ISBN: 978-0-9991989-4-0

Coverart by Basic Bear eBook Extraordinary Designs

Copyedited by Carol Buckley

Foreword by the Editors:

The anthology *Magic, Mystery, and Murder* grew out of the first Coronado Writers Workshop in 2014, when several participating authors requested a regular writing group meeting at the Coronado Library. Susan Enowitz, the conference organizer and cultural commissioner of Coronado, found a time and a space: the second Thursday of each month at the Coronado Library's conference room. The 2nd Thursday Writers group was born and met for three-and-a-half years. Many authors came and went, but April Baldrich, Cornelia Feye, and Tamara Merrill were there from the beginning to the end. Our stories had no theme or connection, until we discovered a common preference for the macabre and supernatural. *Magic, Mystery, and Murder* became our battle cry.

The 2nd Thursday Writers pride themselves on their lack of rules and therefore the order of stories doesn't follow a strict set of guidelines. Instead, we attempted to present a collection of short stories that can be read in order, loosely connected by intuitive links, sometimes just by contrast. A very short story is followed by a long one; a story about a dragonfly is followed by one about early birds, and a story about a beach at summer solstice is followed by one about a lunar eclipse in the desert. We hope the reader will enjoy reading the anthology as much as we enjoyed putting it together.

Cornelia Feye and Tamara Merrill
    September 2017

CONTENTS

1

DO YOU BELIEVE IN GHOSTS?

CORNELIA FEYE

At seven, Stevie was the ghost expert of our family. He knew about the Winchester Mystery House in San Jose, several haunted Scottish castles, and the Whaley House in San Diego. He had two invisible friends and claimed that a ghost lived in his bedroom closet at home.

He was the one who noticed the dilapidated sign for the Hotel Wasserschloss Bonau near Dresden. On spindly wire legs it stuck in the soggy ground and displayed a hand-drawn picture of a moat and castle.

"Mom, can we go to the water castle?" Stevie pleaded.

"What's a water castle?" asked his brother Daniel.

"It's a castle with water around it, dummy," said Stevie.

"Don't call your bother dummy," I told him.

"Maybe it's not a bad idea," their father said. "We have been driving all day."

"Okay, let's check it out," I said. "Time to get out of the car and stretch our legs."

We followed the signs along a rural road until it turned into a trail facing a swamp. Backtracking on the narrow dirt lane, we reached a crossroads on the small country road. Searching for directions, Stevie found one of the Wasserschloss signs. It was covered by weeds and had fallen over on the shoulder of the road.

"It points this way," he declared triumphantly. Obediently we followed the maze-like road through a desolate countryside under a leaden sky. Fewer and fewer buildings dotted the wooded landscape. After what seemed like hours, the road ended in front of a gray two-story castle surrounded by water and connected to the empty parking lot by a drawbridge.

"A real castle," the boys shouted and ran toward the granite structure. We entered the dark empty lobby through a heavy wooden door.

"Anybody here?" my husband called.

A red-haired woman descended the wooden staircase. "Are you here to stay the night?" she asked.

"Do you have room?"

The woman laughed. "You are the only guests; you can choose any room you like."

"Okay, let's pick one."

We chose a corner room on the second floor, with a view of the moat and the woods beyond, furnished with heavy wooden furniture. The red-haired hotel manager told us that the foundation of the castle went back to the 13th century, when it belonged to robber barons. The original castle burnt down, was rebuilt in the 18th century, and then renovated in the 1980s as a hotel. For dinner she recommended a garden restaurant that served wild boar meat, and promised to place two extra beds for the boys in our accommodations.

After feasting on the wild meat and a variety of unfamiliar forest mushrooms, we returned to the dark and deserted castle. We got in with our skeleton keys, and the boys stretched out on their cots and went to sleep.

The double bed was too short for my husband and me, and we lay awake listening to the sounds of the night: birds, the wind in the trees, and a loose shutter. Why were we the only guests in this big castle?

Around midnight a scratching sound right in front of our door and woke us from a light sleep. A woman's voice wailed in a high-pitched, piercing screech.

"Do you hear this?" my husband asked and reached for my hand.

"It sounds like a woman crying."

"What should we do?"

"Maybe she needs help."

"Are you crazy? I am not opening this door."

Was this my husband, the scientist, speaking?

Another voice, low and tortured, joined in. Its deep and desperate moans traveled through the hallway, past our door and upstairs to the attic—a drawn-out howl moving through space.

"There are two of them," I whispered.

"Are the boys sleeping?"

"Let's not wake them," I said. *How could they sleep through this commotion?*

"I am not waking them; those ghosts out there are making all the noise," my husband said.

"Who says they are ghosts?" I asked.

A third voice joined the chorus, sobbing in sharp, short shrieks of agony and anguish. "There is another one," he remarked.

"What is happening?" Terror crept up my spine. We moved closer together, holding onto each other with tense hands, slithering deeper under the blanket.

A fourth voice rose and fell in pitch. One moment it was right in front of our door, then far away, as if muffled by thick walls. It sounded resigned but also as if the ghosts were unable to keep the horror suppressed, erupting in low, long wails.

The wailing went on and on, coming closer, faster, farther, louder. The horror of the voices took hold of us. We watched the door, watched the boys, unable to move. A beam of light came through the crack below the door. The room temperature dropped. It was freezing cold; all the warmth had been sucked away.

"What if the ghosts come in here?" my husband worried.

"There are no ghosts," I said, trying to assure both of us.

The full chorus of four distinct voices erupted again, swelling and fading, moving and flowing, up and down, left to right.

"What do you call this then?" he asked. I had no explanation.

"They sound tortured," I murmured. "Didn't the woman say this used to be a knight's castle in the Middle Ages?"

"This is the twenty-first century," he hissed.

"Maybe their souls ..."

"Don't talk to me about souls. I am looking for the Bible," he interrupted.

There was no Bible in the nightstand or anywhere else. This was part of East Germany, a Communist, atheistic country. "Of course there is no Bible," I said as a chill ran down my spine.

~

Daniel woke up and crawled into bed with us, shivering. At last our ghost expert, Stevie, awoke and assessed the shrieking voices. "What can we do?" I asked desperately.

"We have to seal the crack," Stevie demanded with authority. Obediently I got up and tiptoed to the bathroom, barefoot on the ice-cold floor. I stuffed several towels along the bottom of the door. The chill of the floor crept up my legs. When it reached my knee, I jumped back onto the bed with a gasp before it rose any higher.

The howling continued, until daybreak. At least it was muffled and the temperature seemed to rise a bit. At dawn we heard the last ghostly wails of tormented voices, resisting their departure. Finally, the morning light broke their spell.

~

Breakfast was served downstairs in the medieval vaults. A feast of soft-boiled eggs, freshly baked crunchy rolls, homemade jams, ham, cheese, and an assortment of fruits laid out just for us. The red-haired woman wished us "Guten Morgen" in front of the laden table.

"Good morning," said my husband. "What were those noises last night?"

"What noises?" she asked with a strangely cheerful falseness.

"She's a witch," whispered Stevie, our expert in supernatural phenomena.

"Be quiet, she can hear you," hissed Daniel.

Stevie nodded in a knowing kind of way.

"Eat," said the woman. "This is all for you."

It looked tempting—too tempting. I picked up a pretzel roll.

"Stop," Stevie shouted. "Don't eat it, Mom!"

I froze. The roll suspended in midair.

"What's the problem?" The red-haired hotel manager laughed. "Do you believe in ghosts?"

2

BRIAN ANDERSON: ALL-AMERICAN

TAMARA MERRILL

"I killed Brian tonight. I picked up that brass lamp we kept on the entry table, and I hit him. I hit him as hard as I could, and I'm glad. He said he'd never let me go, that I'd have to kill him first. So I did." Anne spoke clearly, choosing her words carefully as she continued. "This is not a confession of my sin because I'm not sorry. I am calm and totally sane. I killed him because there was no other way to be free." She glanced down at her hands and then back at the policeman. He waited patiently, waited to hear her story.

Just over six years ago Anne graduated from college with a degree in journalism and came to the big city determined to make her mark on the world. She found a job as a copy editor for a small weekly newspaper and was thrilled to be part of the media. On the Fourth of July the sports editor invited her to a barbecue at his home. She accepted with pleasure. The day was hot and clear, as all July Fourths should be. When Anne arrived, the house and yard were full of people, and in the pool was Brian, Beautiful Brian. He stood out in that crowd like a peacock would in a group of ostriches. Anne walked toward the pool; he saw her, rose up out of the water, and came up the pool stairs to meet her. He smiled. She smiled. Someone introduced them. Anne didn't remember anyone else she met that day.

Brian Anderson was an attractive man, very attractive. Everyone who meets him thinks of him that way. He looks like an all-American athlete, tall and slender, with well-formed limbs. His face is handsome, with symmetrical features. His eyes are hazel and measure the world from under level, smooth, perfectly formed eyebrows. His mouth is firm and hard, a straight line drawn across his face. The cheekbones are high, and his chin is square with just a slight cleft. His hair is thick and shining with health, a sun-streaked blonde. Brian is a prosecuting attorney in the District Attorney's office, a very good prosecuting attorney. He is seen often on television and is much admired for his courage in bringing bad persons to justice.

They were an instant couple. Anne went to Brian's apartment that night, and from then on they were together every day and night.

At first Anne would stop at her apartment after work, change for the evening, pick up clothing for the next day, and go to Brian's apartment to fix dinner. It wasn't long until she'd accumulated enough of her wardrobe in his closet that she returned to her apartment only occasionally. Her cat moved away. Her houseplants began to die. Anne felt she was living out of her purse. Sometimes she found it annoying that Brian was so perfect and so orderly. His socks were always mated with his tie, not merely coordinated, perfectly mated. He rose at six every morning and ran seven miles, always exactly seven miles. He insisted that she leave nothing lying about in his apartment, but it *was* his apartment.

Just as she began to resent the inconvenience, Brian proposed. She was ecstatic. Anne told everyone she'd found her Prince Charming. She knew they were destined to live happily ever after. Anne's parents were thrilled with the match she'd made and did everything they could to make her wedding perfect.

Brian's family flew in from out of state. Anne was surprised by how stiff and formal Brian was with his parents. Unlike her family, not a single hug was exchanged when they met at the airport. Brian did kiss his mother on the cheek and shake hands with his father, but there was none of the open, affectionate, rowdiness of Anne's family, where hugs, kisses, and extravagant compliments were the order of the day. Brian's mother reminded Anne of her very strict third grade teacher. His mother was polite but managed to convey her disapproval of everything from the gowns Anne had chosen (wrong color) to the way Anne walked (like a cowboy). Brian laughed and told Anne not to worry, that his mother would grow to love her the same way he had. Anne felt as gawky as a ten-year-old and considered calling off the wedding. But Brian reassured her, and they managed to laugh together.

Brian wanted the honeymoon to be a surprise. He arranged everything without consulting Anne or her mother. He took her to beautiful cabin located on a secluded lake. A lovely little speedboat bobbed at their dock and Brian immediately suggested a swim. Anne managed to stammer "I can't."

"Can't? Can't what?"

"Go for a swim. I don't know how to swim."

Brian shook his head in disgust. "Of course, you can. Even a dummy can swim." He held up a skimpy bikini. "Put this on and let's go."

Anne shook her head. "I can't, I really can't." She started to cry. "I'm afraid, Brian. I can't go in the water, and I can't go on the boat. Water terrifies me."

"That's ridiculous. If you're so afraid, why didn't you ever mention it? I told you my idea of a great vacation was water, water, and more water, that I loved to swim and water-ski. Why did you lie?"

"I didn't lie," Anne protested. "You never asked me what kind of honeymoon I wanted."

"So, now it's my fault? All I wanted was to give you a perfect honeymoon."

"You can go swimming and waterskiing. I'll just watch from the shore."

"And who do you think will drive the boat while I ski?" He turned away and left the cabin, slamming the door behind him.

Anne wept until he returned. She apologized, and he just shook his head and said, "Right." The remainder of the honeymoon week was spent in careful conversation. At night they stayed on opposite sides of the wide bed, and when Anne reached out to touch Brian he turned his back and fell instantly to sleep. At last, on the way home, Brian forgave her, saying, "I don't care that you ruined our honeymoon with your silly phobia. Let's just forget about it." Anne agreed, grateful to move past the argument.

Back in the city they established how to live. They rose together, and while Brian ran Anne showered. Then Brian showered and Anne made breakfast. Always the same breakfast: orange juice (six ounces), two pieces of whole wheat toast, two 3-minute (exactly 3-minute) eggs and one cup of coffee, black, served in his college mug. One morning, when Anne served coffee in a new mug, Brian became angry and began to lecture Anne on her erratic eating habits and on the need to eat regular, well-balanced meals in order to keep an orderly mind. "You must get organized. Your desk is a disaster; you are always behind schedule with your work and with your household responsibilities. Breakfast is the only meal you seem to be able to prepare on time. You need to grow up, Anne."

Anne stared at him in silence for a moment and then blasted Brian with her own complaints about his controlling, superior attitude. The fight that ensued resulted in two days of silence after which Anne apologized and promised to try to do better. And she did try. She carefully cooked the "proper" breakfast, and after Brian left for work at eight-thirty each morning, she quickly did the household chores and hurried to her office to collect her new assignments and turn in her completed articles. Anne planned and shopped for dinner, cooked and made sure that the food was ready and on the table at 7 p.m. Life settled into a routine, and they were happy together again.

Anne had stopped asking for more time-consuming assignments at work. After all she was spending eighteen out of every twenty-four hours learning to be a wife. But, with life finally under control, she wanted a challenge, and her boss gave her one. He assigned Anne to write a series of articles on the new nightlife in the old downtown area of the city. She was excited and planned a special dinner with wine to celebrate. When she blurted out her news to Brian his reaction was not what she'd expected.

"No wife of mine is going to go into that neighborhood and flirt with a bunch of bums," he declared.

"What are you talking about?" Anne could feel her temper rise and she struggled to control it. "Who said anything about flirting? This is great assignment, and it just so happens I love my job and I want to write this series of articles."

"It's not your job. Your job is to be my wife, to be home when I'm home, to take care of my house and to take care of me."

"If you need to be taken care of, why don't you go home to your mother and let her take care of you?" Anne was so angry that she started to cry. "You knew I loved my job when we got married. I thought you were proud of my career."

"Pecking away at your computer, writing gossip for some weekly newspaper is hardly a career," Brian declared coldly.

Anne's tears ceased at once. She stared at Brian, her mouth open in amazement. She tried to make sense of his words. They'd been together for almost three years, married for seven months, and she did not recognize herself or the person she called her husband.

"My mother never worked, and no wife of mine needs to work. If you want to play around and pretend to be a writer, fine. Do it. But do it when it won't interfere with our marriage." He continued talking, but Anne didn't hear his words, just the sound of his voice. She heard hurt—and fear. *He thinks I'm deserting him. He doesn't think I love him.* She apologized for upsetting him and promised she'd ask her boss for a different assignment. Brian insisted that he loved her and that all he wanted was to make her happy.

Anne called her mother and talked to her about Brian's reaction. Her mother assured her that it was a typical male response and that Anne should decide where her priorities were; was it more important to have a career as a writer or to be a wife and mother? And, if her priority was Brian and marriage then she needed to tell him or, even more important, show him. Anne argued that she should be able to have both a career and a marriage, but her mother just kept repeating "I know that's what they say, but in reality it is seldom possible."

Brian was still Anne's dream man, and she was sure she loved him and wanted to be married to him for the rest of her life, to be the mother of his children. She told her boss that Brian couldn't handle the nightlife story, and he told her they'd call her the next time the paper was in need of an extra recipe.

Anne told Brian she loved him dearly and wanted to be a good wife. She changed her routine. Her days were now centered on Brian. She searched for recipes and prepared meals he would enjoy, kept the apartment scrupulously clean, and entertained the business associates he wanted to impress. Anne became the perfect corporate wife, and she almost managed to convince herself that she enjoyed it and was happy. Sometimes she thought about how much she'd loved journalism and how she'd dreamed of winning a Pulitzer Prize for writing something of world-saving significance, but she pushed those thoughts aside and concentrated on Brian.

Anne became pregnant, and Brian was delighted. He was sure that she would have a boy, the exact image of him. They bought a house in the suburbs. Brian bragged to his friends about his clever wife, who decorated the house without the help of a designer, but to

Anne he complained about the chairs being uncomfortable and the kitchen being too colorful.

Anne miscarried.

Brian raged about her careless behavior but quickly apologized and assured her that he didn't really think it was her fault and that they would try again. Anne forgave him; after all he was as upset about losing the baby as she was.

Life in the suburbs was boring and unfulfilling. Anne's mother told her to be grateful that she had such a good marriage, such a wonderful husband, so much freedom. The other women in the neighborhood, who were stay-at-home wives like her, had small children and activities to fill their days. Her former friends had somehow vanished from her life. She turned to daytime television and started to let the housework slide. One night after dinner, Anne admitted to Brian, "I feel like I'm turning into a vegetable. I miss working and I miss living in the city. It's been months since I saw my friends."

"And I suppose you think that's my fault," Brian sneered. "If your friends wanted to see you, they'd call you. You need to pull yourself together." Anne flinched at his words; she wondered if he was right.

"How in the world do you think you could manage a job?" he continued. "You don't keep this place clean. You haven't cooked a decent meal in weeks, and I can't even remember the last time you had it together enough that I could bring guests home."

He turned away in disgust.

Anne decided things had to change. Her marriage was in trouble, and she believed it was her fault. It had been weeks, or maybe months, since Brian had said "I love you" or given her a compliment. In fact, she admitted to herself, she wasn't sure how long it had been since she had said "I love you" to Brian. She began to get up in the morning and prepare breakfast. She forced herself to clean up the house, to dress in nice clothes, and put on makeup before he returned from work. At first Brian seemed skeptical, but then he began to talk to her over dinner and she felt her spirits rise.

Now when she drove to the grocery she looked around and realized the world was still beautiful. She noticed individuals, not just the mothers with new babies but everyone. She began to talk to people. Her quick trips to the store lengthened into all-afternoon trips to the shopping center and then into afternoons at the park or walking in the zoo. Talking to strangers—of all ages—made Anne aware of the part of herself she'd suppressed. She realized how much she enjoyed listening to people and took to carrying her iPad with her so she could write quick character sketches. She began to think of article ideas and wondered if she might actually begin the novel she'd always thought she would write "someday." Anne was thinking for herself again and using her talent for the first time since she'd given up her job to please Brian. The more alive Anne felt, the more she came to understand that she'd given away too much of herself. She wanted that self back.

It was easier to write in a park or a coffee shop than at home, and soon she was talking to other regulars in those places. Anne felt that she was creating friends and a new life. When Brian saw that Anne had "come to her senses," he became happier and less angry and impatient. Anne's mother complimented her on "getting it together." Anne didn't explain to either of them that she was meeting new people and writing every day; instead, she hurried through her chores and left the house as quickly as possible, returning only minutes before Brian returned in the evening.

Her secret was bound to be discovered. On a Thursday afternoon, Anne pulled her car into the driveway and saw that Brian's car was already parked in the garage. She readied an excuse and entered the house.

Brian's angry voice attacked her. "Where have you been?" he shouted.

"I was at the mall and lost track of time," Anne answered calmly. "I was trying to find a new dress to wear Saturday night for your dinner thing. But nothing I tried on seemed quite right."

"I suppose you expect me to believe you've been shopping all day and you didn't buy a thing. I'm not that stupid, Anne. I've been calling this house and your cell phone since ten minutes past nine this morning. I demand to know where you've been and what you've been doing." Brian flushed face was twisted in anger. His fingers were gripping the edge of the kitchen table so tightly that his knuckles were white.

Anne saw her phone on the kitchen counter, where she must have forgotten it in her haste to get out of the house. She berated herself for her carelessness but decided that honesty would be the best policy and plunged into an explanation. She told him about how much better she felt, about her days walking around the city, talking to strangers, and about sitting in the coffeehouse—about how exciting it was for her to be writing again and meeting people, going places, and doing things.

Brian seemed to be listening. Anne was thrilled. She relaxed and began to tell a story about one of the regulars in the coffee shop, a young man who was there every day with his baby. She saw his face change. He was no longer just angry, he was furious. His fist clenched and he raised it. Anne instinctively ducked; she thought he was going to hit her, but instead he slammed his fist into the wall, cracking the plaster and causing a picture to crash to the floor. He stormed out of the room, turning only once as he pulled the door open. Brian glared at her and spat out "Slut!" The door slammed. Anne burst into tears.

She cried and raged against herself, and then, between one sob and the next, Anne realized that she was crying only out of fear. She didn't care that Brian was angry. Anne was glad that she had told him what was really going on in her life. After all, she reasoned, I don't want a marriage where there is no honesty.

What she wanted was a way out of her marriage, a divorce. As Anne calmed down and was able to think clearly, she admitted that the idea of a divorce wasn't anything new. Somewhere in her subconscious she had already accepted the idea.

Anne was flooded by relief. Her tears dried.

She straightened the house, fixed a sandwich, and tried to read. Several hours passed and she began to worry. Whenever they had any fight, Brian always walked out, but he always came back within an hour, two at the most, ready for Anne's apology. Perhaps, she thought, this time he knows that things are different, that I have no need to apologize. Anne wondered if she should call someone, but she couldn't think of anywhere he'd go or anyone he'd be likely to talk to and, she admitted to herself, he'd hate it if she told anyone they'd been fighting.

The evening dragged along and about ten-thirty Anne went in to take a shower. The water sluiced over her body, taking away the knots of tension. She stood under the hot spray a long time, relaxing and letting her thoughts wander.

Suddenly, Brian was shouting, "Come out of there, you bitch! I know your lover's in there with you. Get your ass out here."

Anne reached to open the glass doors, scared to death. As they began to slide open, Brian hit the doors with the chair from Anne's dressing table. With a tremendous crash, the doors blew apart. Immediately she was covered with glass, sharp naillike pieces pierced her skin. Blood began to flow freely down her body. Anne didn't move. Brian froze. He stared at Anne, amazed at what he had done, frightened by the blood.

Anne fainted.

When Anne regained consciousness, she was already in the emergency room. The doctor was putting stitches into a deep cut in her arm. "There, there," he murmured when he discovered she was awake. "You're a very lucky young lady. You have a slight concussion and a lot of cuts, but your face has only superficial wounds. You'll probably have no scars at all on your face. How in the world did you manage to take such a nasty fall?"

"Fall?" Anne asked, confused by the question.

"Yes, how did you manage to fall through the shower doors? Slip on the soap?" asked a nurse.

Anne was furious but her first thought was to cover up for Brian; he'd been angry and drunk, surely he hadn't really meant to harm her. "I guess I must have," Anne answered sheepishly. "I really don't seem to remember exactly how it happened."

The doctor gave Anne a thoughtful look. "Are you sure you fell, Mrs. Anderson?"

She wanted to tell him the truth. But she was ashamed and she stuck to the lie.

"Okay, then," the doctor finished his stitching and applied the last bandage. "You'll be as good as new in a few days. Come into the office on Tuesday, and I'll check to be sure there is no infection. You'll be uncomfortable, so I'll give you something to help you sleep tonight. If you have much pain or need someone to talk to, you call this number anytime." He handed Anne a card and gave her a long searching look and a squeeze on her shoulder. As they left the room Anne heard him say to the nurse "Fall, my eye." And the nurse responded, "I know, but what can you do?" Anne hoped Brian hadn't overheard them.

Back at the house, Anne didn't insist that Brian leave. Only hours earlier, she had confessed to herself that divorce was the best—only —answer, and yet she found herself forgiving him. He was so repentant. He had cried on the way home, something Anne had never seen him do before. She reached out and touched his hand.

Brian looked frightened as he turned toward her and pleaded, "Anne, I'm so sorry. I don't know what got into me. I love you. Please forgive me." Anne sat in silence, but he continued, "Please don't hate me. I don't want you to leave me."

"Brian, I don't hate you. I love you, but I can't understand why you were so angry. You know I wasn't with anyone else. Don't cry anymore, and we'll talk."

Brian helped her change into a nightgown and then carefully tucked her into bed. He pulled the duvet over Anne's aching body and made a cup of her favorite raspberry tea. He was gentle and tender and very solicitous. They talked for hours. Anne believed him when he said he would never again let his temper get out of control, that he never meant to harm her or frighten her. Anne told him how important her writing had become and how much she wanted to go back to work. Brian swore that he understood.

They promised that they would never keep secrets again, that they would be more open and loving to one another. Anne never mentioned divorce, and Brian never withdrew the jealous accusation he had hurled through the shower door. Anne didn't notice. She drifted off to sleep secure in their love, sure that the problems of the past were resolved. She just needed to be sure that she always showed Brian how much she loved him.

The following week, when the stitches came out, the doctor again gave Anne an opening to talk about what had really happened. She avoided his questions about her safety and stuck to the same fall-in-the-shower story. The doctor didn't seem to buy it, and as Anne was leaving he gave her a pamphlet about a crisis center for battered women. Anne still didn't say anything, but before she started her car she sat in the parking lot and read the section entitled "Ten Red Flags that a Woman Is Being Abused." She really didn't believe that any of them described her. She threw the folder into the glove compartment and drove home.

Only a few days later Anne planned a roast for dinner. She put it in the oven, and since her stitches were gone and the bruising was covered by her clothing, she went for a walk, stopped at the coffee shop, said hi to a couple of people and was home before Brian. Dinner was ready on time, but the roast was a bit overdone. Brian took one bite and said, "What happened to this meat? It's terrible."

Anne laughed. "It's not that bad. I was busy. Put some gravy on it and pretend you like it well done."

Brian stood up so fast his chair tipped over with a crash, and he stood towering over Anne, clutching the table with both hands. "There is nothing funny about the roast, Anne. You were out having fun, with God only knows who, this afternoon, weren't you? You couldn't even be bothered to take the time to make a decent dinner. What kind of wife are you?"

He moved away from the table and came toward Anne. She began to tremble, her thoughts raced. Was he going to hit her? She jumped up and turned to run. Brian grabbed her hair. The sudden pain stopped her forward motion. She stumbled. Brian's fist slammed into the small of her back and she dropped to the floor, her arm crumpled under at an odd angle. Anne screamed at the pain from the breaking bone.

Her scream seemed to bring Brian to his senses. He fell to his knees, moaning, "Oh God, what have I done? Annie, are you all right?"

"Get away from me!" Anne screamed. "Don't touch me." She pulled herself up with her good arm. "I hate you. I hate you. I hate you." The words reverberated from every corner of the house. "Go away. Leave me alone. I hate you." She stumbled into the living room and reached for her phone. Brian caught her hand.

"Please don't tell anyone, Annie. It was just an accident. I didn't mean to hurt you. I just wanted you to listen to me. I love you, you know I do."

"You certainly have a strange way of showing it." Anne was calmer already. She didn't really want to have to tell people she'd been hurt in a fight with her husband. She watched him carefully, but he didn't attempt to move toward her. She thought about how she'd laughed at him, and she admitted to herself she was at least partially to blame. She was ashamed. "Okay, I won't call anyone, but after you take me to the emergency room, I want you to get out of this house, tonight. I don't want to be alone with you right now."

Anne cradled her arm in the car and didn't say anything, not asking why Brian drove to a different hospital and declared that they had no insurance but he'd pay cash. The doctor who attended her didn't blink at her story of falling down the stairs. He put a cast on her arm and told her to go to her regular physician, or return to the outpatient clinic, the next day for a cast check. At this hospital she was just one of many and no one asked any questions or gave her concerned looks.

Brian kept his word and left the house as soon as she was inside, but he was back before breakfast the next morning with a huge bouquet of roses and more apologies. Anne was no longer afraid, but she stayed firm in her resolve and didn't allow him back in the house. He courted her. Every day he courted her with phone calls and presents and invitations. Soon Anne gave in and they went out to dinner.

With Anne's arm still in a cast, Brian was helpful and sweet, helping her off with her coat and cutting her steak. Their waitress commented on how lucky Anne was to have such a great guy and, at Brian's request, snapped a picture of them. That dinner was the beginning of a chain of lunches, dinners, walks, and movies, and every time they were together they talked. Brian spoke candidly about his insecurities, the feelings of jealousy he experienced when Anne was busy with work or others, and he vowed he had changed. It seemed to Anne that they brought everything out into the open. They grew closer than they had been during their courtship.

And so, after six weeks, they were living together again. Her mother told Anne that she was glad she had "come to her senses." His parents didn't comment, and Anne wondered briefly if Brian had told him they were separated. Her friends were thrilled; not only was Anne spending time with them again, the perfect couple had reunited. Love triumphed.

Brian had agreed to see a marriage counselor, but somehow neither of them ever managed to make the appointment. Anne's arm healed. Brian hadn't lost his temper. Things were so good there didn't seem to be a need.

A few weeks later they were invited to a party. It was a large, rather formal affair and Anne was looking forward to it. She bought a beautiful dress and had her hair blown out. Brian told her she was beautiful, and she told him he was, too. They left the house in a festive mood. Their marriage had been running smoothly for almost three months. Anne was considering suggesting that she go back to work. They were young and in love; life was glorious.

The party was one of those bubbling affairs where conversations sparkle and flow, where everyone has a good time. Anne drifted from group to group, talking and laughing with friends she hadn't seen in months. Brian was also circulating and laughing. Anne thought about how much fun they would have lying in bed later talking about everyone: who'd been there, how they'd looked, and what they'd done and said. The party drifted to a close. Anne chattered in the car, not noticing that Brian was silent. They entered the house and Brian slammed the door. Anne turned, surprised at the sound, then stunned at the look on his face.

"Well, you certainly had a good time, didn't you?" he asked nastily.

"Yes, I did. Didn't you?"

"How could I possibly have a good time with my wife making a spectacle of herself?"

"Brian, I did no such thing. I thought you were having a good time, too. Every time I looked you seemed to be talking and laughing." His eyes narrowed and he glared at Anne as she continued, "What in the world are you angry about? Those people are our friends; of course, I talked to them."

He started toward her, and suddenly Anne understood the true meaning of terror. Her body turned to ice. Her heart pounded. But she knew she'd never let him hurt her again. "Brian," she said firmly, "if you touch me I'll scream. I'll scream so loud the neighbors will hear."

"So what?" he sneered. "Do you think they'll come to your rescue? If anyone can hear you, which I doubt, they'll just think the nice young couple next door is into something a little kinky tonight."

He came closer. She wanted only to escape. Anne spun quickly and ran toward the door. Brian was faster. He leaned on the door, smiling at her. "Going somewhere?"

I hate him, Anne thought. *I truly hate him. It isn't that I dislike him and I'm not angry, I truly hate him.* The strength of the emotion stopped her panic and she spoke calmly. "I hate you, Brian. You're a mean, spiteful man, and I don't want to be married to you anymore."

He slapped her.

Anne didn't even flinch. "Get out of the way. I'm leaving you."

"Bitch." He spit at her. Anne recoiled. His hand flashed out and this time the slap snapped her head back. "I'll never give you a divorce. You'll have to kill me first."

"Is that really what you want me to do?"

He smiled, that horrible superior, I'm better than you smile. The smile that Anne used to think was so perfect. "You wouldn't dare," he stated calmly.

The months of their marriage roared through her head, one memory after another, all the anger, all the fear, all the love that wasn't love but was only control. Anne was ready to leave, and this time she wouldn't change her mind. "Brian," she said firmly, "I'm walking out that door and I never want to see you again."

He hit her then, not another slap, but a blow to her stomach with his fist. She dropped to her knees, her head cracked against the table, and the brass lamp crashed to the floor. Anne grasped the lamp and staggered to her feet. "I mean it, Brian. Let me go."

He laughed. "Never."

Anne swung the lamp. There was a dull *thunk* as it connected with his head. Blood spurted out of a gash above his eye. He looked bewildered, and crashed to the floor, unconscious.

Anne stepped over his body.

"Goodbye, Brian," she said, opening the door and allowing it to slam behind her. She walked slowly toward her car, started the engine, bucked her seatbelt, and drove carefully to the police station.

3
***

ALBAN HERUIN SUMMER SOLSTICE

APRIL BALDRICH

The bonfire burned through the summer night's haze, creating a pocket of smoky clarity. Another summer season was welcomed by young revelers along the shores of the Pacific Ocean. Clad in hooded sweatshirts, and armed with red Solo cups, they splashed and danced to the rhythm of the solstice. The night when the veil between the mortal and spirit world is briefly lifted— allowing a glimpse for souls that long for connection to the other side.

I opted for a solitary walk along the bluffs, a bottle of my favorite lager in the pocket of my Carhartt jacket. The waves crashed furiously against the rocks, a sound akin to the smashing glass of the high-speed accident. The invigorating ocean breeze did little to lift the oppressive sadness, which, of late, weighed heavily on my soul. No closer to peace, I descended the staircase down the cliffside to join the party on the beach.

I opened my lager and sat by the fire pit, feeling no warmth. The party went on around me. Several young women I had never much cared for danced clumsily near the fire, singing and laughing. Another group sat in front of a guitarist while they braided hair and passed a joint. Their names escaped my memory. Young men tossed a football in the breakers, attempting to catch the attention of the dancing girls. All were engrossed in life, as it had been—enjoying that moment. How I envied them.

Turning my gaze toward the cliff, I noticed a large, solitary rock. I walked over and perched myself on top, drawing my legs to my chest, bare feet securing my balance. My green eyes stared pensively at the party. As the marine layer rolled in like opium smoke, I was overcome by a wave of nostalgia.

I sat there remembering the summers past. Everyone, here at the beach—like old times, so young and carefree—their whole life ahead of them and full of possibility. I just wanted to capture this halcyon dream. This is how I wanted to remember them—forever.

Out of the corner of my eye, I saw my brother, Shay, approaching.

"Carli?" he said hesitantly.

We looked the same; nothing had changed since we'd last seen each other.

"Carli, why are you up here being an antisocial weirdo?"

All I could do in response was stare in disbelief, as my body tensed, bracing itself against the pressure of gushing tears.

Smiling, Shay balanced himself beside me on the rock. "What's your deal, lil' sis?"

I grabbed for his arm, searching for substance, as if it could hold me to this world. Competing with my sobs for breath, I spoke spastically through my tears. "You're ... going ... to ... to be gone ... soon. You're ... all ... going to-to be gone. There isn't much time left."

Shay eluded my grasp by jumping off the rock, landing on the powdery sand, hued white by the moonlight.

"Carli, I don't know what the hell you're talking about. You're always going off by yourself, like a selfish child. You're not the only one that has feelings and thoughts. This party may be over soon, but it's happening right now. I'm here right now. Why waste time crying about the dawn when the sun hasn't set?"

With that he turned and walked toward the party, taking his place among them.

I was alone on the rock. The bonfire was dying down, and the party fading with it. One by one the bodies and objects of life vanished from the beach.

4

LUNAR ECLIPSE

CORNELIA FEYE

Vega and Greg sit in the shade, by Red Willow Creek behind Taos Pueblo. Tourists are not allowed here, but they don't consider themselves tourists, even though they travel around in a rental car and camp in a tent. They're here on a mission.

They are not alone at the river. Two young Taos Indians sit on logs and drink beer. Apparently the ban on alcohol is not strictly observed on the reservation. The Pueblo Indians do not seem to mind the urban looking couple, in their slightly grungy clothes, sitting by their river.

One of them lights a joint and passes it to Greg.

"Where you from?" he asks.

"New York," Greg answers. "We live in Brooklyn."

"Never been. Never been farther than Albuquerque. I'd like to go to New York one day." He doesn't sound urgent.

"You live in the pueblo?" Greg asks.

"Nah. The pueblo out there is just for the tourists. I live in a house on the rez."

"My name's Greg."

"Garrett, Jimmy." He nods toward his companion.

"What you guys doing here? Just taking in the sights?" asks Jimmy, who wears his black hair in a ponytail.

"I am doing research on Navajo sand paintings," Vega explains.

"No Navajos around here. You gotta go to their Arizona rez. We and the Navajo don't get along too well."

Vega nods. She knows about the bad blood between Pueblo Indians and Navajo, who arrived in the Southwest only 500 years ago and spoke an Athabascan language of different origin from the Pueblo languages. The Navajo displaced many Pueblo cultures and took their land. Now the Navajo occupy the nation's biggest reservation. Vega says nothing. She does not want to state the obvious or dwell on a delicate subject.

"We had to come and see Taos Pueblo. It is the most beautiful of them all," she says instead.

The two almost smile.

"It's been here a lot longer than the Navajo." Apparently Jimmy cannot let go of the subject.

"Where you staying?" Garrett asks.

"At the campground over at Red River. We saw the lunar eclipse there last night. It was amazing," Vega says.

Both shake their heads.

"None of us looked at that. It's very bad luck for men to see a lunar eclipse," Garrett declares with a fierce look in Greg's direction. Greg shrinks under the piercing stare.

"It's okay for women?" Vega asks.

"Yeah, it's okay for women," Jimmy says dismissively.

They sit in silence for a moment. The joint starts to have its effect. Time seems to flow by as slowly as the Red Willow Creek. Insects buzz and a low swish of a tail floats over from across the river, where three horses graze.

"Are these your horses?" Greg asks.

"Yep, the small brown one is Blueberry. He is faster than he looks," Jimmy says.

"You wanna go for a ride?"

Greg shakes his head vigorously. "Bareback? No way."

"We could just ride over to Garrett's house and show you some contemporary Pueblo art," Jimmy tempts.

The words *Pueblo art* do it for Vega. Of course they have to go.

"Is it far?" she asks, seeing Greg's extremely hesitant expression.

"No, just a few minutes," assures Garrett. "You can share a horse."

"Share a horse without saddle or bridle?" Greg is highly alarmed. "I don't even know how to ride with a saddle."

"It's easy. The horses know the way," Jimmy says.

"Let's just go for a little bit," Vega pleads. "It will be so interesting."

Maybe it is the joint, maybe he does not want to chicken out in front of the Pueblo Indians, but Greg agrees against his better judgment.

They wade across the creek, and Garrett helps them onto the biggest horse, named Rusty. It feels very high. Jimmy mounts Blueberry, and Garrett rides a red horse named Fox.

They trot up the hill and enter onto an open field strewn with boulders and shrub. So far so good. Suddenly Vega hears Jimmy whisper, "Let's go, Blueberry."

As if stung by a bee, Blueberry takes off in a stretched gallop, disappearing across the terrain like a brown streak. Fox and Rusty only hesitate a moment, before following in full pursuit.

"Whoa!" Greg screams behind Vega, leans forward and tries to grasp the horse's mane, but he has nothing to hold onto.

"Hold onto me," she yells as they fly across the rock-studded area, not a path in sight. Without saddle, they bounce up and down on the horse's broad back. The ground looks very far away and treacherous as pointy rocks and thorny brush fly by underneath Rusty's hooves.

"What do we do?" Greg shouts.

"Slow down," she screams, but Blueberry, Fox, and their riders are so far ahead, they do not hear them, and Rusty races to catch up.

"A tree," Vega calls. "Grab onto a branch of a tree and get off."

No big trees in sight, just a few low cottonwoods. When Rusty approaches one of them, Vega ducks down low not to hit her head and Greg tries to grab a branch and lift himself off the horse, but the branch breaks and he loses his balance. Vega sees him slip, feels him slide as he goes down hard. She hears him hit the ground with a sickening thump as his head hits a rock.

"Greg!" she screams.

She has to get off this gigantic horse, has to slide off somehow, since there is no way to stop it. Searching the ground for a patch without rocks, she leans sideways off the horse's neck and lets herself fall off, rolls over, and comes to a halt. Her left shoulder is bruised, scratched, and bloody in the sleeveless shirt, but at least she has solid ground under her feet.

"Greg!" she scrambles up and runs back to where he has fallen.

"Help!" she yells, holding Greg's bleeding head in her lap.

Jimmy, Garrett, and their horse are long gone. Silence and empty land envelops them. Vega has a flashback of New York, where there is always an ambulance with a blaring siren within earshot.

"Greg, are you okay? Can you hear me? We will get you out of here," she promises, as much to herself as to her companion, who is only half conscious. "It will be okay." She is crying now and tries to stop the bleeding with her bandana. *Where is everybody? The pueblo is close*, she thinks, *so there must be people around*. In the distance she sees an old Jeep driving across the rough terrain.

"I am getting help, Greg. Just lie here for a moment." She beds his head on a smooth rock and jumps up, waving wildly.

"Over here!" she screams. "Help!"

A wrinkled, old Taos resident drives up, loads both of them into the backseat and takes them to the hospital in Taos without a word. Vega is not sure whether he has observed the accident, but he asks no questions. She is grateful and tells him so. He only nods and silently drops them off at the emergency entrance.

Greg gets patched up with twenty-two stitches to his head. He is lucky, the wound is superficial. Next to his bed lies another patient, who has been hit by lightning.

The patient looks over at the heavily bandaged Greg and asks: "Did you also look at the lunar eclipse last night?"

After a couple of hours, the hospital releases them with a bottle of hydrogen peroxide, extra bandages, and Band-Aids for Vega's scratched shoulder. They take a taxi to pick up their rental car at the pueblo and drive back to their campsite, battered, bruised, and weary in torn, dirty clothes and with aching limbs.

"Damn horses," Greg finally says.

Vega sighs. "I am so sorry, Greg. I should not have encouraged you to ride them."

"Especially not without a saddle," he agrees.

"How are you feeling?"

"Lousy. But it was not all your fault. I mounted that monster of a horse after all."

For a few moments they drive silently on the empty, tree-lined road.

"I feel like such an idiot," Vega finally says.

"A couple of New York idiots in New Mexico," Greg confirms.

"You think they did this on purpose?"

"Of course. You heard how Jimmy spurred on his horse Blueberry to a gallop."

"They were both untamed."

"They were teaching a couple of stupid gringos a lesson."

"Maybe it has something to do with the lunar eclipse," Vega suggests.

Greg looks at her sideways. "You seem to be okay."

"It does not affect women."

"I don't want to talk about this. My head hurts."

Two days of changing bandages, applying hydrogen peroxide, and resting is all they need to recover enough to pack up and drive to the Navajo reservation in Arizona. They turn off the freeway and on a five-mile gravel road they reach the Navajo trading post in Rough Rock. Vega takes photographs and examines the rugs, with sand painting motifs, woven by local Navajo women.

"This is a Snake Way ceremony rug," Vega explains to Greg. "The women change the design from the original, because it is sacred and cannot be seen by outsiders. The sand painting is destroyed after each ceremony."

Greg nods. He has heard it before.

The Navajo girl behind the counter chews gum with a bored expression. She apparently has already determined that these two visitors are not going to buy an expensive Navajo rug.

"What happened to your head?" she asks Greg, who still wears a white ring of bandages.

"I fell off a horse," he says.

"The day after the lunar eclipse," Vega adds to see if this gets a reaction.

The girl nods knowingly. "That happens to guys. Shouldn't have watched it."

"We are looking for a Navajo medicine man to put it right," says Vega.

The girl looks at them appraisingly.

"Kenneth Yazzie is a *hataalii*. He lives down the road, about fifteen miles from here. His hogan is not easy to find, but I can draw you a map."

She draws on the back of her receipt block. "After eight miles, you'll see two small windmills pumping water, on the right of the dirt road. Take a left there and follow the road for another seven miles up the hill. It's rough going. I hope your car can handle it." She hands them the piece of paper.

"Thank you very much," Vega says. "Should we call ahead?"

The Navajo girl looks at them with disbelief, shakes her head, and turns her back to them. Maybe she already regrets giving these ignorant city people so much information.

"You can't call, but you should bring gifts," she says as she turns and places two cartons of cigarettes and three 6-packs of soda on the counter.

Back in the car with their loot, Vega is so excited she can barely contain herself.

"Can you believe we are going to meet a real *hataalii*. Maybe we can ask him to do a sand painting ceremony for you. That would be incredible! White people are hardly ever allowed to see that."

Greg is driving and mumbles "Another wild adventure, if we ever make it to this medicine man. This road is terrible, and I have no idea what we'll do if we blow a tire or get stuck in these ruts."

"We'll just walk the last part of the way. That's more respectful anyway."

"You suggest we walk the last ten miles?"

"Oh Greg, it's all about your head. This will make you feel better."

"I am not so sure I trust these Navajo, but I think it will make you feel better."

"This is what we came for. It was all meant to be."

They pass the windmills, pass a shepherd, who nods vaguely in the western direction when Vega calls the Navajo greeting *Yá'át'ééh* and asks about Kenneth Yazzie. As the road disintegrates into a riverbed with deep ruts between sharp rocks, Greg finally refuses to drive any farther. Clusters of houses appear on the ridge above, and guessing they may belong to the Yazzie clan, they walk uphill carrying their plastic bags of soda and cigarettes. They seem to weigh a ton in the heat of the day. Panting and sweating, they reach the top, and Vega spots a dome-shaped structure, made of wood covered with mud, showing an entrance opening to the east.

"We must be at the right place. This is a traditional ceremonial hogan of the Diné, the Navajo people. We have to wait here until someone comes out."

"I hope they come out soon, because my head is throbbing."

"I know, but this is why we are here, to make you better," Vega says excitedly, and Greg realizes his bandaged head is her entrance ticket to this hogan and its medicine man.

A young man comes out.

"Yá'át'ééh," Vega says.

The young man says nothing.

"We have come to see Kenneth Yazzie, the *hataalii.*"

He looks at her silently, waiting. Vega understands that the conversation has to be conducted slowly and without impatience, even though she feels the urgency and knows Greg is not going to stand here and wait in the heat forever.

"We brought gifts," she says and hands him the bags. "Tobacco and drinks."

He nods and takes the bags.

"My friend has fallen off a horse and hurt his head the day after the lunar eclipse," Vega continues. "We come from far away, from New York, for a healing ceremony."

The young man still looks at her expressionless. Vega is not even sure if he understands her, but finally he nods and motions with his head to follow him to the hogan.

Inside, the structure is cool and dark with a single round opening in the middle of the roof. A shaft of bright daylight pours in. The hogan is empty except for a cot along the wall, where an old man with crutches sits next to a woman—the medicine man and his wife. On the opposite side of the hogan, an old Navajo couple sits on the floor on a blanket. Vega assumes they are patients, because the woman wears a grimy bandage around her wrist and hand.

Vega and Greg are motioned to sit on the ground, and the young man kneels next to the medicine man and speaks to him in Navajo, pointing toward Greg. The old man looks at Greg. He nods eventually, and the young man waves them to follow him to a trailer nearby, where they are led to a cluttered kitchen full of people.

"Wait here," the young man tells them and leaves.

Glad to be out of the sun, Greg sits down on a stool and drinks water. Vega sits next to him and smiles at the people in the room—teenagers, young girls, boys—all looking at them. They fell silent the moment Greg and Vega entered.

"Áą', how are you?" Vega asks timidly.

They don't answer, but begin to talk again and move around the cramped space.

"You are here for a healing ceremony with my grandfather?" one of the girls in tight jeans asks.

"Yes, a healing ceremony for his head." Vega points to Greg's bandages as if his wounds can lend their presence legitimacy. It seems to work.

The young man returns.

"I am Vega, and this is Greg," she introduces.

"Ben," he says. "Kenneth Yazzie's grandson."

He leads them out into the desert. The medicine man awaits them, sitting on a blanket facing north, his crutches beside him. Ben tells them that his grandfather will perform the Earth Prayer ceremony for them and asks them how much they want to contribute. They each give him a couple of twenties, which he takes without expression.

"What about the hogan and the sand painting?" Vega whispers to Greg.

"Shhh," he hisses back as the old man begins to chant in the Navajo language.

Ben sits to the side and shakes a rattle in a monotonous beat, while his grandfather opens his medicine bundle and removes two fetishes wrapped with wool and topped with feathers. He hands one to Vega and one to Greg.

Vega holds her feather bundle tensely. She has not come all this way just for an Earth Prayer ceremony on a bluff in the desert.

Nervously she looks around. The land stretches empty in all directions, from the top of the ridge, over tan boulders and gentle dunes, to a great expanse studded with mesquite shrub and stunted cottonwoods. A slight breeze blows from the north; the fetish's feathers tickle her hand. She barely notices. The vast dome of the sky, uninterrupted by telephone poles or man-made structures, spans the axis of heaven. She looks over at Greg, but he gazes straight ahead, calm, at peace, in the moment. Vega takes a deep breath and tries to relax.

Kenneth Yazzie opens a small pouch and takes out pinches of corn pollen he places into their palms. He shows them to put some on their tongue, their head, and their heart for a blessing, then lets the rest of the pollen blow away in the wind. He chants, and from another pouch he pulls out blue cornmeal for their tongue, head, heart, arms, and legs, allows the wind to blow it away. Vega sees Greg's eyes follow the tiny cloud of cornmeal as it disappears and dissipates over the ridge. She notices that the medicine man has stopped his chant. He packs his fetishes and pouches back into his bundle. Apparently, the ceremony is over, after half an hour.

As their small procession walks back to the houses, Vega cannot hide her disappointment.

"What about the sand painting ceremony in the hogan?" she asks Ben.

He raises an eyebrow and cocks his head sideways. Greg jabs her in the ribs.

"Please, thank your grandfather for this beautiful blessing ceremony," she says quickly. "It's just that we were hoping ..."

Ben waves her back into the trailer to the chaotic kitchen. Vega sighs and accepts one of the sodas they brought.

"Wait here," Ben says and leaves them again.

Vega looks at Greg who appears maddeningly calm. She decides to make some conversation. Maybe she can at least find out some information from the inhabitants of this cluttered home. The people milling around don't seem interested in their guests and are unimpressed that they have come all the way from New York, even though one of the younger children admits that nobody from so far away has ever made it to their settlement.

Finally Ben returns.

"Come," he says and leads them to the hogan, where he tells them to sit down.

While they attended their Earth Prayer ceremony, the medicine man's wife has laid out a Snake Way sand painting on the floor of the hogan with multicolored sand. Four snakes have been drawn in white, black, yellow, and blue outlined in complementary colors for the four directions. They are surrounded by a rainbow border in the shape of an incredibly stretched rainbow deity. Her body arches around the four snakes, feet at one end of the rainbow and head almost touching its other end in the east. Vega gasps.

Greg touches her faintly at the elbow and smiles, as if to say "Now are you finally happy?"

Vega nods, ecstatic to be allowed to observe this ancient ritual. The ceremony begins for the old woman with the bandaged hand. Obviously she has been bitten by a snake. Vega is relieved to see that she still wears the plastic wristband from the hospital. Medical care first; spiritual care second.

The ritual unfolds in front of them in the shifting, slanted light from the circular opening on top of the hogan. The patient is led around the room three times in clockwise direction, while the medicine man chants and his wife shakes the rattle. The old woman sits on the sand painting facing east and repeats the chant, line by line. Ben comes in and brings her yucca suds to drink. He puts liquid on her arms, legs, neck, and breasts. The old man walks around her and chants over her, while she holds black and green feather fetishes.

The repetitive chanting lulls Vega and Greg into a meditative trancelike state. Time slows as the sounds seem to stretch and a shaft of light from the opening becomes the center of the world for this moment only—everything and everybody revolve around it.

At the peak of the ceremony, the patient takes off her blouse. Sand from the painting on the ground is transferred to her body—sand from the head of the snake to her head, sand from the snake's body to her chest—the transfer of sacred sand to her sick body to replace poison with blessing.

Ben goes outside again and brings smoldering pieces of coal and incense in a tin can. He places them on the right side of the patient and holds her hurt hand into the sweet-smelling smoke. He shoves the smoke all over her body for purification, with chants and prayers that accelerate in tempo and increase in volume and urgency. The ceremony aims to transform her whole being. Vega and Greg feel a shift in the air as if the renewal has affected not only the patient, but even the sound, the light, and the occupants in the hogan. Time stands still in this moment of transformation.

At the completion of the ceremony the *hataalii* conjures the restoration to beauty and harmony.

"With beauty before me,
With beauty behind me,
With beauty above me,
With beauty below me,
With beauty all around me," the medicine man chants in Navajo.

Kenneth Yazzie, his wife, and the patient have exhausted themselves. The old medicine woman brushes the smudged sand painting together into a blanket and takes it outside. It will be discarded and buried, since it now has absorbed all the poison and sickness of the patient.

Suddenly the hogan is quiet. The patient puts on her blouse and looks around as if uncertain of where she is. Vega and Greg feel the same way. They are not in the same space they entered, and they are not the same persons they were when the ceremony began. Shaking themselves out of their trance, they try to return to the present from a state of suspension between two worlds. The old man lies down on his cot, and his grandson tells them it is time to go.

They leave the hogan not knowing how long they have been inside, lost in a timeless space. Crawling out of the low door feels like emerging from a womb back into the world, still wobbly on their feet. Their eyes have to adjust to the brilliance of the sun going down over the golden hills in the west, in the blazing red of sunset. A half moon is rising over the horizon in the east, just a normal moon, swimming in front of a flaming red desert sky, suspended harmlessly over the black silhouette of the mountain ridge. They walk silently down to their car.

"How do you feel?" Vega asks, nervous that Greg did not feel the intensity of the ceremony or was not as moved by its power as she was.

"Good. Peaceful." He takes her hand. She sighs a deep breath of relief. Apparently he has forgiven her for leading him into, and then out of this crazy adventure.

"Is your head better than before?"

"Before the fall or before the ceremony?" Greg tries to clarify.

"Is it better than before the fall?"

"Yes, I feel better than before the fall."

Vega squeezes his hand.

In their car, they open the windows to let in the warm evening air and follow the moon to their campground. They don't need to talk, because the silence of the night carries the blessing that connects everything.

5

ERRONEOUS PERCEPTIONS

TAMARA MERRILL

"If I knew where to find a cliff, I'd take this dumb thing and drive if over the edge." Lisa kicked the flat rear tire of her old, blue SUV and tossed her head, causing her long blond hair to blow across her face. She tucked the loose hair behind her ears and kicked the tire again. Lisa grinned ruefully at Janet. "Well, what do we do now? I don't have the faintest idea of how to change a tire, and I doubt that much traffic is going to wander down this road." She pursed her lips into a pout. "Me and my dumb ideas."

Janet couldn't help but laugh. "Lisa, we've been in bigger trouble than this a dozen times. Sometimes I think I've only kept you as my best friend all these years for the excitement. You and your crazy impulses have been getting us into tight places ever since kindergarten. Besides I wanted to come to the desert as much as you did."

"I know, but I'm the one that insisted on driving my car even though I know you take better care of yours than I do. And," she shrugged, "besides the flat tire, I think we're lost. I haven't been able to figure out which direction the freeway is from here for almost an hour. I've just been driving around hoping to get a cell signal on my phone, or that something would look familiar."

"You did seem a little preoccupied, but I thought you were just figuring out some fantastically clever way to use some of those this-tles we picked." Janet slipped off her jacket and opened the car door. "Okay, open up the back of this thing and let's dig out the spare. We can figure this out. I've watched guys change flats a few times, and it didn't look that difficult. Lucky thing I'm wearing these old jeans or I'd make you do it yourself."

Lisa smiled at Janet. "You're always so capable. You look like a fairy princess, with your gorgeous hair and your perfect tiny body and yet you're standing there, hands on your hips, ready for action and sure you can handle it. How come?"

"Don't start analyzing me, Lisa, just open up the back and let's change the tire and find our way home." Janet moved to the back and Lisa followed.

She studied the spare tire and an assortment of loose parts for a few moments, then rolled up the sleeves of her delicate, frilly shirt and set to work.

Lisa sat on the sand and watched in amazement. "Are you positive you've never done this before?"

"Lisa, I appreciate your awe but, for heaven's sake, there's really nothing to changing a tire. After all there's only one place to attach it. It's not exactly a puzzle." Janet swiped a dirty hand across her fore-head, leaving a smudge. "If I can get this damn thing off, I'll be able to get the spare on. Get over here and help me turn this 'wenchy' thing."

Lisa wasn't much help, but between them they were finally able to loosen the lug nuts and get the tire changed. As Janet finished and reloaded the flat and the tools in to the back, Lisa rummaged around in the SUV and found an old T-shirt and a bottle of water. Janet scrubbed at her hands, and, when Lisa pointed, her forehead. She took a long drink of the remaining water, stowed the now T-shirt towel and empty bottle, and headed back to the front. "Come on, let's get out of here. It's going to be dark before long."

Lisa put the key into the ignition, and the SUV roared to life. "Which way do you think I should drive?" she asked.

Janet swiveled to face her. "Lisa Hamilton, are you serious?" A cloud of anxiety passed over Lisa's face, and Janet softened her tone. "You are serious, aren't you? You really don't know where we are."

"I'm sorry. I was having such a good time catching up on all your news, and talking about myself, that I didn't pay any attention after we turned off that little road and headed across the desert."

"It's all right." Janet touched Lisa's hand. "Just stay calm and we'll figure this out. You've been out here before haven't you?"

Lisa nodded. "I love the desert, and I find all kinds of things that I can use to make art, but"—she snuffled a bit and admitted—"I've never driven out of sight of the freeway before. I usually just stay parallel so that I can find my way back."

"It'll be alright. If we drive west, we'll find the freeway, or a road, or a sign, or something."

Lisa looked at Janet, waiting for direction. "West," Janet said. "Drive toward the sunset."

The sky glowed first orange and then red and pink as the sun sank lower and it began to get dark. Janet watched carefully for any sign of lights from the freeway or a town. She constantly checked her cell phone, hoping for a signal so they could get directions from Google Maps. Just as darkness became complete they found a dirt road and turned to follow it, still heading mostly west or perhaps southwest, Janet wasn't sure. "It's really dark out here, isn't it?" she commented.

"It's one of the reasons Jim and I moved to the desert," Lisa admitted. "On a clear night the stars are amazing."

"Can you tell which direction we're driving by looking at the stars?"

"Nah, Jim can. But I don't know anything about them." Lisa took a deep breath. "Do you think we're going the wrong way?"

"I have no idea. We were headed west, but this road has made a few turns. At least we are on a road now, and I'm sure it's going somewhere. Where there's a road there must be people right?" Lisa didn't answer. Janet noticed how tightly Lisa was holding the steering wheel and realized Lisa was afraid. "It's after six. Won't Jim be wondering what happened to us?" she asked.

"He'll wonder where we are, but he won't be mad and he won't worry. He's always pleased when I've been busy all day doing something I like, and he knew we were going to spend the day together." She smiled and relaxed her grip on the wheel. "With any luck, he'll start dinner."

"Excellent. I'm starving."

"You'd better hope he brought home steak, 'cause that's the only thing he knows how to cook."

"Steak will be perfect. After we get back on the freeway how far are we from your house?"

"Not far. I think it's only about twenty miles, maybe a little longer. I'm pretty sure this is the same road we took this afternoon. Does anything about this road look familiar to you?" Lisa turned toward Janet, hope evident in her face.

"I'm such a city girl that all the rocks and cactuses and those twisted trees look the same to me." She took another look at her phone screen. Still no signal, and the battery was down below 20 percent. She switched it off to save the charge. "But, I trust you to find your way home."

Lisa's hands tightened again, and Janet tried to change the subject. "It fascinates me that a girl like you would ever move to a ranch house way out in the desert, with horses and chickens."

Lisa giggled. "Love does strange things to your plans. We can get to downtown San Diego in less than an hour, on a good day, and we don't have any chickens." She glanced at Janet. "I never expected to live this way, but I love it and I love Jim."

"I know you do. I just remember when we used to talk about what we would do when we grew up. You always said you'd live in Manhattan. I think I envy you your life. You seem so ... What's that?"

"What's what?"

"That noise. Listen. Don't you hear a *flump, flump*?"

The SUV sputtered and came to a halt. There was no *flump, flump*. There was no sound at all.

"Shit," Lisa slapped the steering wheel.

The car clicked as it cooled, and then the complete quiet of the desert settled around them and dark night seemed to become darker still. Janet reached over and squeezed Lisa's hand. "It'll be okay," she said, as much to reassure herself as to reassure Lisa. "Somebody is sure to come along this road soon."

"I don't think so. If I'm even sort of right about where we are, this road goes out to a bunch of old, run-down cottages built on the San Diego River. At this time of year no one is going out there or coming back in the middle of the week. If it was a weekend, we might see somebody, but not tonight."

"Don't be such a pessimist. A camper or a rancher or highway patrol or something will come by."

"That's exactly what I'm afraid of."

Janet looked quizzically at Lisa. "What's exactly what you're afraid of?"

"That 'something' will come by. Roll up your window and lock your door."

Janet turned toward Lisa. "What the heck? If someone drives this way we'll be able to see them for miles. It's perfectly flat out here."

"No it isn't. The desert has lots of dips and arroyos where things can hide. And, it's getting darker." She pushed the door-lock button. "People have been murdered in this desert."

"Stop, it Lisa. You're weirding me out. Try to start the car."

The engine made a loud grinding sound and a puff of something that looked suspiciously like smoke rose from the tailpipe. Lisa turned the key again. The car responded with complete silence.

"My phone battery is almost dead. Try your phone."

"I don't have it," Lisa admitted. "I think I left it in the kitchen."

Janet pulled out her phone and powered it on. The low battery warning flashed, but if there was a signal, she could probably make a call. "I've got one bar. Here." She handed the phone to Lisa. "Call Jim."

They could both hear the phone ring and then Jim's voicemail message. At the beep, Lisa said, "Honey, the SUV broke down some-where in the desert. We need you to come and get us. I'm not sure where we are—maybe, that old river cottage road. It's a dirt road. I can't see the freeway from here or any lights. I turned off at the Mountain ..." The phone beeped and went dead.

Lisa handed the phone to Janet. She turned it off and returned it to her pocket. The two young women sat silently starring at the dark desert. Finally, Lisa spoke, "He was probably just in the shower."

Janet nodded. She could see that Lisa was upset. "Relax, sweetie. Everything will be okay. Don't I always bring you home safely?" Janet asked. They laughed together and reminisced about their past escapades. Without cell phones they had had no way to know how late it was getting, or how long they had waited. They reassured one another that Jim would understand Lisa's message and send help.

The night air grew chilly. Lisa had only a beach towel. They moved to the back seat, huddled together, and grew quiet. They dozed.

A tap on the window caused them to jerk awake. "Did you hear that?" Lisa whispered.

Janet nodded. She grabbed Lisa's hand and squeezed it. If Jim was there to rescue them, why was it still dark?

The tap came again. "You alive in there?" a young male voice asked. A flashlight roamed across the SUV's interior and highlighted the women's faces. Janet could feel Lisa shaking.

"Don't worry." The voice sounded as if the speaker were trying not to laugh, "I'm not the Desert Killer. I'm just a guy hiking back to my camp and happened to see your van." The flashlight moved away from them.

Janet sat up and pushed the towel aside. She reached for the door lock. Lisa grabbed her hand. The flashlight was pointed to the man. She could see his jacket and a backpack.

"It's just a guy, Lisa. He can help get us out of here. Maybe he's got a phone."

"And maybe he's the killer."

Janet turned to look out the window again. He'd switched the flashlight off, and she couldn't see anything but his silhouette against the starry sky. "Do you have a cell phone?" she called.

"What? I can't hear you?"

"Cell phone," Janet shouted. "Do you have a cell phone?" He nodded and dug into his jacket pocket.

"Sure," he said. "Want to use it?"

"Yes, please," Janet said politely.

"He wouldn't let me use his phone if he was the killer," she hissed at Lisa and reached to open the door. She stepped out of the van. He looked okay, Janet thought. At least the little she could see of him in the weak glow from his phone's screen seemed normal.

"Sorry," Janet said. "I'm Janet and this is my friend Lisa, she gestured toward Lisa who was still watching from the van.

"Harry," he introduced himself and handed Janet his phone.

Janet handed it to Lisa, saying, "Try your husband again. At least then we'll know if he's on his way."

"Did you already call for help?"

"Yes, quite a long time ago, right about dark, but my phone died."

Lisa waved the phone at Harry. "I don't think this thing is working."

"Let me see; reception out here is pretty spotty. Last time I used it was a couple of hours ago from my campsite." He glanced at the screen. "Sorry, no bars here."

"But my phone worked," Lisa protested.

"Who's your carrier?"

"AT&T."

"That might be it. I'm with Frontier." Harry grinned. "If you give me the number you want to call, I'll try from my campsite or you guys can come back there with me. I have lanterns, food, and a fire." Janet and Lisa exchanged looks. Harry continued, "I'd give you a ride out of here, but I hiked in and my buddy won't be back to pick me up for a couple more days. How far away is your rescue person coming from?"

"A bit west of Temecula," Lisa admitted.

"Whoa, that's at least a couple of hours from here. I can leave you here and go try to call, but it gets pretty cold in the desert at night and I don't have a blanket or anything in my pack."

"Is it a long ways to your camp?" Janet asked.

"About a mile straight west of here. It's not a bad walk." He eyed the suspicious girls. "I'm going over there." He pointed away from the car. "You two decide what you want to do."

Janet was cold and hungry, and she didn't think this Harry guy seemed scary, so she argued that they should go. Lisa argued that they didn't know him and there was a killer on the loose. However, she was cold and hungry, too. They decided to accept his offer.

"Right," Harry said when they told him. "Got something to write on? You can leave a note for whoever finds your car."

Janet dug in her purse and produced both paper and a pen. She scribbled a note and then asked, "How does this sound?"

A guy named Harry found us.
We have gone to his campsite about 1 mile west of here.

"You might want to add that my last name is Olson and that I'll keep a bonfire burning all night so that they can find my campsite."

Janet amended the note and then asked if she could include his cell phone number. "Sure," he said and rattled it off.

Janet placed the note on the dashboard and weighted it down with a rock. The interior light dimed and went out. Lisa pulled the keys from the ignition, slammed and locked the door. She whispered to Janet, "Do you really think this is okay?"

"I don't think we have much choice. Besides he gave us his cell phone number. No bad guy would do that."

"Ready?" Harry asked. The girls nodded. "Stay close; I only have this one flashlight, and there's a lot of stuff to trip over out here." He smiled. "Don't worry, it's just a short walk, maybe half an hour, and you will be warm and cozy by the fire before you know it."

They followed him out into the dark desert night. Quietly and quickly, like sheep to the slaughter.

6

DESERT DREAM

APRIL BALDRICH

After five years in California, my finances, health, and dream of Nobel glory is slipping away. I need a hot meal and a good night's sleep, but with no money in the bank, and finals fast approaching, those luxuries will have to wait. My body and sanity are submitting to the destructive will of my ambition.

I stand in the dusky light of my bedroom. It could be morning or evening. My addled brain has lost all construct of time. The abrasive crank of my alarm clock suggests I have somewhere I need to be. I need a shower.

The warm water and steam do little to refresh me. My unsynchronous mind rambles beyond my control, my empty stomach in knots. I should call my dad, but he won't send money, only smug judgment. I am on my own. My household budget begins rambling through my mind in baseless arithmetic. I convert my late rent from grams to moles. My car payment in Kelvin is greater than zero, but if I calculate my electric bills in joules and titrate the cost of petrol, I could, just maybe, buy some groceries next week.

I'm sweating and nauseous as I fire up the engine of my ancient Honda. Heading north on the freeway, I bypass my exit. Two miles later I light a cigarette and cut east toward the high desert. I drive for hours in silence with the dusty air pouring through my open car windows.

I am somewhere between the Mojave and Death Valley, when the desolate silence is interrupted by the banging of a Honda engine—more specifically, my Honda's engine. The silence quickly returns as my powerless car rolls to a stop on the side of the road. *Fuck. My. Life. Where the hell am I anyway? Why the hell would I take a shitty car into the desert with no cellphone reception and only twenty dollars in my pocket? I am going to die in the desert.*

In the immediate distance I see a weathered wooden building with a baby blue '62 Thunderbird, with the top down, in the parking lot. *Awesome sauce!* Grabbing my water bottle, I embark on the trek. I have no real plan, but I'm cautiously optimistic.

I discover the structure is a roadside bar and carryout. The shutters are closed over the windows, and I struggle to pry open the heavy red door. The bar is dimly lit by a jukebox and a few stained-glass lamps that rely heavily on embossed wall mirrors to perpetuate their glow. In days long past I'm sure this place was filled with smoke, laughter, and the clacking of billiard balls, but today it is just me and two silent pool tables. I take a stool along the brass railing of a varnished bar and stare blankly at the bottles of liquor.

"Sionna?" Hearing my name breaks my trance, and my eyes meet those of a lanky man with a ruddy complexion and matching hair. "Y'er far from home, aren't ye youngin'?" I stare blankly at the vaguely familiar man as he stares back.

"Perhaps y'er answers lay in the bottom of a glass?" h
e asks as he pours me two fingers of Jameson neat.

Realizing I'm staring at him like a ghost, I speak. "I'm sorry. I'm just having a shit day. My life sucks, my car's broke, and I'm lost. And how the hell do you know my name?"

"Aye there, Sionna, I'm not to be remembered by ya, but I know ya well. Y'er not so lost as ya think. Take da drink, it'll do ya."

Lacking the mental strength to flesh out this situation, I put the tumbler of Irish whiskey to my lips and pour it down my throat—acrid with a warm finish, just like my mother.

Setting the empty glass down on the bar, I hear the clacking of billiard balls, the air becomes heavy with smoke, and the room is filled with the laughter and commotion of drunken revelry. The bartender gently takes my hand in his. "Sometimes the solutions we want aren't to be possible. In those moments, ya gather what ya do have and find a new way."

The bartender turns and walks away, my hand trailing his until it slips beyond reach. I am left isolated on a parallel plane. My anxiety mounts as the bar becomes a clamorous blur of color that is squeezing the air out of my chest. I am bumped without acknowledgment by drunken strangers as I spin wildly around searching for a way out. I see a lighted doorway in the back. Crossing my arms over my chest I make my way through it, to a deserted room.

Inside there is only a wooden chair and table, but, most importantly, it is cool and quiet. My hyperventilation comes to rest as I sit in the chair and regather my dissociative thoughts. The silence is broken by the sound of a projector flashing a film reel from a bygone era onto the bare wall.

The Shannon River rolls on the wall. Ireland, nearly a century before—green hills and orange sky. Sky moves to black and the hills to tan as fires burn and women sob tears of mourning and defiance. A young Irishman presents in the swaying barley with his rifle.

There's a cottage, where a frail woman stands fretfully with a small girl—a girl I recognize from pictures as my grandmother. The Irishman, rifle in hand, approaches, dirty and limping. He loads a few worn suitcases into a cart while the frail woman tearfully places flowers by a tiny headstone.

I see them walking up the gangplank of a ship, suitcases in hand, heads hung low, an uncertain life in America ahead of them. The Irishman looks to his family and says, "Sometimes the solutions we want aren't to be possible. In those moments, ya gather what ya do have and find a new way." The projector abruptly shuts off, leaving the room silent and dim.

I need to find the bartender. It was him in the film, my grandfather. Crossing the threshold of the room, I find the bar dark and abandoned—and not recently. The stained-glass fixtures are broken and dusty, as are the remnant furnishings. The jukebox is faded and busted. There are no liquor bottles, just broken boards and broken glass.

I make my way by the scant light shining through the boards covering the windows. Struggling with the door once more, I exit to a brilliant sunset. I see the Thunderbird parked outside. A retreating beam of sun reflects off a chrome keychain dangling from the ignition.

I lean over the driver's side door and turn the key. What can it hurt? The engine turns over like new, and the fuel gauge displays full. Despite the inexplicable situation, I am strangely calm.

Sitting behind the wheel, I look to the south—home and all its futile, demoralizing battles. I turn the wheel of my steel "land boat" to the north and head into the unknown.

7

THE SALAMANDER

MAX FEYE

D eep in the throat of the Mohave, I'm swerving down the desert road like a madman, knowing I'm not going to get out of this alive. I lick the dryness of a hangover away from my lips as my eyes flick to the rearview mirror—a black jeep roars. It maneuvers itself to run me off into the jagged, cracked hills, and I turn away onto the burning sand.

It doesn't take long before I'm stuck in the sinking sands of the open desert. Banging my hands on the steering wheel over and over, I hiss like a wounded animal, my tires spinning and kicking up sand at the men now walking toward my buried car. They let out their ancient bloodthirsty cries of glee into the desert air to echo for miles around, and not a soul will hear. I put my head down on the steering wheel and close my eyes tight. For a second, a strange feeling: remorse. They always say your life flashes before your eyes. It doesn't. V. is the person I see.

Skin slick with blue neon, she glides around the pole, and I sit, nursing a whiskey. Spellbound. So pure, so untouched by the wolfish eyes of the men all around. Gravity doesn't apply to her as she orbits. Venus. The Crystal highs make them feel like gods, king and queen of the desert. I walk into our hotel room and see her teeth kicked in, rose robe splayed out showing bruised nakedness. She didn't deserve what the Chief did to her.

The men outside were sent by the Chief, who runs a dozen of those fake fancy clubs in the southwest corner of Vegas. Really played up the whole Native American thing too, always talking about spirits and sacred animals and shit. Couldn't have been more than a quarter Native, but it added to the mystique. He'd call me for his dirty work, which meant I was never out of a job. A lot of those jobs ended up buried out here in the desert. Now look at me.

I don't know why, but I start to laugh. Even as I'm ripped from the car and onto the hot sand, I howl as I'm beaten by giant leather hands. "Where is the money?" they ask. A shovel is thrust into my hands, and I dig my own grave while they search my car. I skip the begging and the crying for their sake. I always hate when they do that. They'll kill me and we'll be done with it. Someone calls from the car. They've found it.

I'm hit on the back of my head and fall face down into the dirt. An earthquake brews inside my skull. My brain starts to crawl with fire ants and their biting, tearing, and searing; something sounds like rain. No, no, just kill me first. The dirt comes down in waves, the silence in between used to beg out of the corner of my mouth, "Please. Please." The earthy rain pulls me into weighted black.

I can't move. Jesus, I can't move. Panic rises. The weight of the earth is an unrelenting vice grip, the pressure sits, prevents breath, and this inner voice: it's-it's panicked and loud; it drowns out the heartbeat I'm listening for and Jesus! Something cracks. What if I stay like this forever? What if I can't die? Those assholes are standing over me now, are laughing, taking their cut, pissing on my grave, and no one will ever know I'm here, or look for me, and no one cares, or ever did. I need to get out. To get to the open, to breathe, to just move. *MOVE!*

With a force beyond anything I've ever summoned, I pull the dirt away from me. It feels like grabbing the entire universe and ripping it apart.

The earth gives way. Sweet, beautiful movement; I reach toward the loose sediment and pull myself toward it. *GO. GO. Please God. Help me.*

I fall. Down somewhere. And I land hard. A cascade of sand follows suit and covers me. The ghostly echo of pain in my spine is sweet, and quickly disappears. I cough up sand. Lying on my back, my eyes open to white light, illuminating the soft remnants of falling sand and covering me in a glowing spotlight. But the source of light seems so stagnant, so far away. Everything tells me I have to get back up there. With that thought, my senses kick in. The sound of a hundred off-tempo metronomes. Dripping water off the perspiring cave walls creating little pools in the limestone floor. The air is still and cool. I wiggle my fingers. The pain disappears as I get up and explore the darkness in order to get back up to the light.

My eyes struggle to adjust to the complete darkness. I only make out the edges of things, but sometimes they play tricks on me. Color pulls itself out of the dark; violets dance around rocks. A red growls from chasms below. Blues lazily float. They form patterns, moving together. But I ignore them and forge forward until I see the edges of a tunnel, a possible passage out. But the tunnel splits, and soon I find myself facing dozens of different paths. A labyrinth of random choices, one way will split into another three, and I am unsure if I am caught in a loop or if I am making progress. I walk for what seems like miles, in the pitch-blackness, groping the rocks for support. The tunnel gets smaller and smaller; I am on my hands and knees. *Please don't get stuck, please.*

But a burst of cold air hits me. *Yes!* I scramble forward, grabbing out with my hands, like a baby for mother's milk and I pull myself through. An open cavern greets me. Cracks line the ceiling, ancient vents that bring a dim light to the space. Stalactites drip from the ceiling, each new drop building the stalagmites on the floor. In the center of the room is a giant column, where, after an eon of trying, the cave floor and ceiling finally met. It draws me in with its ancient glow. I run my fingers over its smooth ridges.

"Hey."

I turn around, looking into the blackness. Had they followed me down here?

"No, not there, dummy. Up here."

I turn to look up and see a slimy translucent salamander cocking its head at me. It has no eyes, only strange reddish gills.

"Good to see you again."

I don't know what to say. The strangeness overrides my brain.

"You ... can't be real."

"If you say so."

"So are you?"

"I don't know, probably."

"You don't know if you are real?"

"Do you?" The question feels like a dagger against my throat.

"There's a way out of here, you know."

"How?"

"Well there are two, actually. You can either go left or right."

"But they both lead out?"

"Technically, yes."

"What's left?"

To the left is a small hole in the wall. It looks dark and uninviting.

"Emptiness."

"And to the right?"

There is an opening in the wall, coated in a dancing blue light.

"...Well there's light that way. But just because you can see doesn't mean you'll like what you see."

The choice seems obvious. I'm headed toward the light. The salamander's eyeless gaze follows me. I can barely hear his last words.

"Great seeing you again."

I spin around and see the bare rocky column. No salamander. I need to get out of here, before the dark starts creating more of these strange hallucinations. I forge on.

The source of the blue light of the tunnel is an abundance of beautiful crystal growths. However, they are razor sharp, and they dig into me as I squeeze through the narrower sections. But I don't care. I just want the light, that beautiful natural light to shine on my face. I want to pull myself out of this place and back into the world.

I've been the poisoned meat, filling every person I touch with sickness and pain. The violence, the money, all the girls. What was the point of it all? To feel like a man? The silence down here is changing me; I need noise to shut out this voice and these thoughts. *Forget it. Forge on.*

The cave opens up into another giant expanse. I walk down a natural path of angled limestone that winds its way around crystals in delicate and intricate formations. A scuttling noise cuts through the silence.

A centipede forges a path over sharp crystal. It crawls onto an emerging island of rock and slithers up the heel of a red stiletto, moving up to a smooth tattooed leg, and disappears behind V. She looks at me as if I gave her the world.

"Take me with you, baby."

"V. How did you—?"

Scanning for a path to her over the sea of crystals, I'm stranded.

"Come to me."

"I can't"

"Crawl."

I want nothing more than to be with her, to hold her; I really do.

"You never loved me, did you?"

My throat is swelling up, and my eyes burn. I can't answer. It feels like my heart is splitting in two, separated by a sea of sharp glowing crystals. I can't handle this. What is this feeling?

Standing there with his arm around her is the Chief. His long hair is braided, and as always he is wearing his jewel-studded cowboy-style bolo tie. They look at each other warmly and proudly before he speaks.

"You were like a son to me. Our spirits have travelled together for thousands of years; I'm sure of it."

I rub my eyes. *Jesus, am I crying?* I look up and see a pregnant woman standing where V was before and a man with a thick moustache next to her. She smiles warmly while the man rubs the woman's belly. They look at me.

I can't take this anymore. I turn and run from them. That's all I ever knew how to do. I can't face them, not here, not ever.

As I run back the way I came, the glow of the crystals flickers and dims. They have lost their sharp edge. As I stumble into them, they are fragile and they shatter.

I have now returned to the column. The toothed room is comforting if only for the fact that I know I am not lost. But I am desperate to get out of here. The salamander is nowhere to be found. I look toward the other path, the hole in the wall. I sprint into it and I fall. Down and down and down. Haven't hit the bottom yet, losing consciousness. The wind whipping in my ears fades.

I open my eyes to a galaxy of small bluish lights. Stars. Twinkling lights surround me, stretching to infinity. Above and below, I am floating in a cosmic expanse. I sit up, suspended in time and in awe of the beauty and scale of it all. *Where am I? Am I dead?* It is the most beautiful thing I've ever seen.

I get up and take a step toward the closest star. I look down as I do so, half thinking I might plunge into the depths, spiraling without gravity into the cosmos. But I step on a perfectly still thin layer of water that covers the floor. My step sends ripples through the water, shaking every star to its core. The entire universe below me is thrown into disarray. *I disrupted the balance, I have disrupted the beauty.* I feel the dawn of something beautiful on the horizon of my mind. A thought, like the tiny remembrance of a dream. A dream as old as all these stars. A realization that maybe if I stay real still, if I fight the urge to run, that maybe I can stay in this strange void, I can become one with it. The thought slips away as I see a light in the distance, like a dream woken from.

The light is on the horizon below the stars. It emits the comfort of home, of life, warm and vibrant and bright. The same light I fell down from. I miss the light so much. I wish it hadn't come to this. I want to start over. These thoughts have become so loud and so strange as the silence and the dark wrap around my mind. I take another step and throw the stars into chaos again. I don't care, this time. I walk forward and the water gets deeper, the white light gets larger, closer. I see a star hanging above. It is some sort of a worm, with a bluish light in its tail. It is surrounded by a web, reflecting its light and creating a matrix of illumination. I am surrounded by hundreds of thousands of these. Moving, living things creating this universe. The white light grows bigger. I am swimming now. No thoughts but that light. It is so beautiful. It's all I want.

I dive down, because the light is submerged. *Yes, yes, yes a million times yes.* Away from the darkness, I'm swimming my hardest, with everything I have and more. But it is still too far away. I'm running out of air. My heart is bursting, my lungs fighting for oxygen. Had I even been breathing this whole time? I have to breathe.

My lungs fill with water, but still I struggle. *I won't make it. Please. To be this close and . . .* my brain is losing these words. Not enough oxygen. Curl into fetal position. Glowing light. Brighter.

The baby boy slides out into the nurse's arms. Crying, the naked child screams the amniotic fluid out of his lungs. A mustached man looks down with love and pride. He holds his newborn son in his arms while his exhausted wife smiles.

Shapes, colors, and sounds all flood the baby's senses as the time spent in the dark and silence slips away, the image of a blind salamander just a faded dream.

8

HERE BUT GONE

KATE PORTER

W e each cross our legs, right over left. My hands remain safely stowed under my thighs until I sweep hair from my eyes. His hair has receded to nothing, so he rakes fingers through a beard—the closest thing he can do to mirror my move.

Are we in sync? Maybe.

Rocking on the porch swing, we sway like parakeets. Our silence is stunning, save for the gentle *swoosh* of our perch. The sun streams under the bougainvillea to bake my knees exposed below my shorts. Testing for sunburn, my finger pushes on the skin—blood drains. Releasing the pressure—blood rushes back. My knee smolders just like my anger.

Is this man really my father? Maybe.

A dragonfly appears and alights on my burnt knee. I know it is a she because I maintain a love affair with insects, which began in high school and persists. Back then, life was simple: catch a bug, identify it, kill it in formaldehyde, stick a pin through its thorax, and mount it in a wooden bug coffin. Now, life is complicated: husband, kids, house, bills, and all their never-ending complexities. Why then has this creature, in a simple act, chosen my warm skin as the spot for an afternoon rest?

Nature could be alerting me to the synchronicity of earth, sky, wind, and love.

I look at the man beside me and at the bags under his eyes. He isn't the perfect father specimen I'd imagined, but I have found him, and he is the only one I'll have. I imagine the formaldehyde and the giant pin necessary to keep this being in place.

The dragonfly tickles my skin. As a teenager, I composed poetry in my head. That was twenty years ago, but writing poetry is like riding a bicycle. When learning how, it keeps dumping you on the pavement, but you can't help but get back up for more. Poetic phrases begin to pop like firefly flashes in my brain.

> A red-bodied helicopter
> with silver wings as see-through
> as lace tat-tat-tat tatted
> she lugs a massive twitching head
> windshield eye wrap-around windows
> reflecting all colors seeing all things
> a rainbow world
> Oops, gone in a flash

She takes off, and my mind is back to hunting for something to say to this man, my father. He glances at me, and a slight smile appears on his lips. Again, she lands on the exact spot as though it is home. Poetry returns.

> Returning to this warm surface
> a sunny knee blushed with pink
> she wears a brick-colored hairy wrap
> her thin tail tattooed with black
> she stands still but pumps
> up and down, up and down

Father is breathing in the same rhythm—in and out, in and out. Should I call him "Dad," even though it doesn't feel right? Am I ready to forgive that he abandoned Mom to raise me, alone? A second dragonfly arrives.

A male darts into view
his colors flashing green
he flies backward does a 180
returns and docks upon the knee
Will he stay? A moment later
Oops, he's gone in a flash

She's alone
    her legs as dainty as black twigs with feet
    four down and two up she paws the air
    reaches to smell a fly a mosquito a gnat
    multitudes to eat today her jaws will gnash
    Oops, she's gone in a flash

Back again
    he hovers silent flying perfection
    at thirty beats per second
    he flutters above this planet above this knee
    will he make contact?
    Oops, gone in a flash

"Are you okay?" my father asks, attempting to make contact.

I notice his cigarette breath, too close, and wipe a tear from my cheek. "Just watching those dragonflies," I say. "Did you see them?"

"No," he answers and scans the air by swiveling side to side. His searching intensifies. "My wife says I never notice anything." He sighs. He gives up.

Tears speed down my cheeks. I need him to be someone who will notice me, who will never give up even though his wife is not my mom. Realizing I have no patience for a man who isn't aware of more than his own thoughts, I sigh. I give up. "I don't think I'm ready to have you in my life."

He shakes his head. "I was afraid of that. Do you want me to go?"

There's been no apology. Calling him "Dad" feels risky, but I decide to try it once. "Look, Dad, I'm thirty-eight, and you never looked for me. I don't know where we go from here."

"I'm not going anywhere," he says and reaches for my hand.

As though shooing away a flying pest, I brush his hand away. Then I stand up, run down the porch, and leap off the steps.

"Gone in a flash," he calls out.

I stop. We are in sync. The earth spins below, clouds drift across the sky, and a fierce wind arrives at my back to shove me forward, away from him. But I don't move. I can't move. My feet feel planted in indecision. Risk, a burden bolstered by the past, weighs on my shoulders. I turn to face him. He's standing on the porch edge. I will not go to him even though his arms reach toward me. Will he cross this distance between us? He won't.

"Not yet," I say, swivel, sprint away, and nearly take off in flight.

A selection from Kate Porter's novel, *The Vagrant Darter*

9

EARLY BIRDS

CLAIRE RANN

The morning starts like any other. The sun creeps into the sky later with each day, much to Zinnia's disdain. Unfair that the change of the seasons should punish early risers. Daylight savings would end soon enough, but until then, she is stuck with the dark and the cold.

She sips her coffee and nurses her oatmeal as she mentally rehearses each step of the surgery she'll be leading in a few hours. Just an appendectomy, sadly, nothing exciting, but it's her first go at lead surgeon, and there's no room for error.

She clatters her bowl into the deep metal sink more loudly that she needs to, hoping the noise startles Mother awake. Mother's barely left her bedroom since the funeral. That was three days ago, Zinnia thinks, jaw tensed. Her father would not have wanted them to use his death as an excuse for sloth.

Not that Mother had ever needed an excuse. Even when Zinnia was little, while she and Father took long hikes through the canyons, Mother slept in every weekend. They'd return at noon to find her still curled up in bed.

"Arthur and Zinnia, my little early worms," she'd greeted them once, crumbs from her half-eaten muffin dusting the sheets.

"Early birds," Zinnia corrected.

Father laughed. "Yes, I doubt there's much benefit to being an early worm. Just more breakfast for the early birds."

"You two," said Mother. "Such dark senses of humor."

The house shudders as Zinnia shuts the heavy front door and heads for her car. It wasn't just their senses of humor that set them apart—it was the way they saw the world. Father and Zinnia made and kept commitments, alphabetized their bookshelves, ironed their clothes for the week ahead. Not like Mother, always running late, half-finished watercolors and barely started novels cluttering her office. And all her feelings, her tears and causes and passions that bubbled up from nowhere and dissipated just as quickly.

"This will all be too much for your mother to handle," Father said after he received the lymphoma diagnosis. He asked her to move home. Zinnia resented how he bent himself to Mother's whims and weaknesses, but his reliance on Zinnia mattered more. Especially once she realized what his plans were.

Zinnia's foot hitting something hard and unexpected at the door's base jolts her back to the present. Another foil-topped casserole littering the porch. Neighbors had been leaving them dishes and Saran-Wrapped bowls, as if the Morrises' kitchen appliances had stopped functioning rather than a family member.

She nudges it to the side and continues to her car. The neighbors are just like Mother, eagerly seeking any opportunity for drama. Father had been much better at suffering fools than her, Zinnia thinks as she backs out of the driveway. What else could explain his twenty-five year marriage to Mother? Zinnia assumed he'd taken an anthropological interest in her. She saw it in the way he looked at her when she arrived home beaming with some impulse buy or brilliant story idea. As Mother babbled on, he'd stand considering her, head cocked, the edges of his lips curled in amusement.

Zinnia's tongue feels sandpapery and thick as she waits to pull onto the freeway. Traffic, even at this hour. She takes another sip of coffee from her travel mug. The world is working against her this morning.

Her thoughts clear and sharpen as she eases down the on-ramp. Like Father, she can will her focus to the matter at hand, clearing away all the clutter that obscures minds like Mother's. Even while dying, Father managed to keep sight of what mattered.

How different the world would be, Zinnia thinks as she changes lanes, if everyone else were more like the early birds.

Zinnia exits through the same gray metal doors she'd entered just forty-five minutes before, wrenching them open so hard the handles thud and ricochet against the wall.

By the time she'd arrived at the hospital, the strange sensation in her mouth had become a throbbing burn, her tongue angry and red when she consulted a mirror in the bathroom. It felt enormous, its seething edges spilling over her bottom set of teeth. Her tongue too swollen to speak, she grabbed a notepad to explain the situation to her attending. She wouldn't be allowed to lead the surgery, but she was certain they'd still need her for some other role.

Can't talk. Probably an allergic reaction, she wrote. *Not contagious.* She underlined that part and handed the notepad to Dr. Hix, her attending.

"Open up," said Hix. Humiliation stung through Zinnia as she complied, heat flashing again when he made a face at the sight of her tongue.

"Go home," he said. "Get some rest."

I'm fine, she scrawled on the page. *I can still assist.*

"Zinnia, go home," he said more firmly, his eyes rounded with concern. "You should still be out on bereavement anyway."

His patronizing tone infuriated her. This unwelcome pity, this insipid insistence of others that she lean into weakness and let it reign. Another resident attempted to pat her shoulder as she turned to leave, but Zinnia bristled at the touch and continued on her way.

Father was the only one who would have understood her need to simply do what needed to be done. Pragmatic to the end, he'd been showing her his most recent round of alterations to the garden when they breached the topic of his death. Zinnia had always been his second-in-command in the garden, Mother barely able to remember to water the houseplants weekly. Where the red sage bushes once had been now stood an odd-looking evergreen.

"Planted this after the doctor told me they'd have to run more tests," he said, pointing to the small, shrub like, tree. It seemed out of place, its branches outstretched in upward V's that gave it a frantic appearance, like an excitable child.

"Yew trees last for centuries," he said. "People plant them in graveyards to watch over the dead. Superstitious beings, we humans are."

"Not us," said Zinnia.

His pupils met hers. "Nearly every part of the yew is extremely poisonous. Quick to kill. Difficult to trace."

She fingered a branch, feeling the dry prickles against her skin. "When?"

"Before I become a burden, lose my capacities." He looks toward the house. "Your mother wouldn't understand, but it's best for everyone this way. Do not involve her."

After the chemo took all his hair and ceased to stop the tumors' growth, after he could no longer hold up a book or remember what he'd eaten for breakfast, Zinnia knew it was time. In the early morning darkness, she plucked bark and a handful of needles from the tree, ground them up, and added them to a tea bag.

At his hospital bed, when she handed him a white paper cup of tea instead of his usual silver-lidded mug, she could tell he knew. She wouldn't be careless enough to leave behind any evidence.

She knew, too, that he would wait to drink it until she and Mother had left, and as Mother sat beside him, stroking the one bony shoulder sticking out from under his papery gown, something in her stomach sank and wrenched. It was time, though. She reminded Mother of the visiting hours' nearing end, and the plants at home that needed tending.

"Yes, go, water the garden before it gets too dark," Father quietly insisted. "They shouldn't suffer in my absence." His face had hollowed, mottled dark circles prominent around his eyes.

"Bye," said Zinnia, and she found herself shaking slightly as she squeezed his gaunt hand. This is what needs to be done, she reminded herself. His skin seemed translucent. It didn't feel like skin anymore, but something softer, more tenuous.

"I'll pluck a little bouquet to bring you tomorrow," Mother said, smiling as she stood up to kiss his forehead.

Zinnia resisted the urge to roll her eyes at Mother's suggestion, knowing that her father would not want murdered flowers by his bedside. It wouldn't matter anyway. He wouldn't be here in the morning.

He is gone, Zinnia reminds herself, cursing the water building around her eyes' edges as she turns onto their street. But he'd died on his own terms, when his living ceased to bring him purpose. It's sad, of course it is, and Zinnia misses the only person for whom she never needed explanation, but what's the use of dwelling in that sadness? Nesting in bed may bring Mother some solace, but for Zinnia the only relief is staying focused on what's in front of her, if the world would just let her.

Zinnia pulls into the driveway, her shoulders rigid and pinched. She lets herself into the back gate. She will sit in the garden until her fury subsides.

"You're home early." Mother's voice surprises her. She sits at the small wooden table beside Father's pots of basil and thyme and other herbs. The potted leopard lily, usually next to the front door, sits at the table's center. Strange, Zinnia thinks. It's an indoor plant, shouldn't be out here. She shrugs and changes direction to return to the house.

"What's the matter?" Mother asks. "Cat got your tongue?"

Zinnia stops. Mother's eyebrows are arched, taunting.

"Didn't you notice your coffee tasted a little different this morning?" She takes a sip from her tumbler. "You're not the only one who knows things about Arthur's plants."

She'd done this. Zinnia's hands instinctively go to her neck, her throat now throbbing. How much longer did she have? What could she do? Thoughts swirl as panic sets in, but Zinnia is frozen.

"Dumb cane is another name for leopard lilies, you know," Mother says. "Arthur always loved them but wouldn't keep them in the house 'til you were older."

Zinnia's fingers curl and tighten into white-knuckled fists at her sides. Even after Father's death, Mother finds a way to interfere, to ruin the things they'd held dear. She wants to lunge toward her, rip the graying hairs from Mother's head, but her legs are heavy and weak, her breath labored.

"It was the only way I could get you to listen," Mother continues. "After what you and Father did, it's the least I can ask."

Zinnia's forehead wrinkles. She'd been so careful.

"You would never bring him tea in a paper cup," Mother says, as if reading her mind. "Entirely wasteful," she continues, perfectly parroting Father's tone. Her voice softens. "He loved that mug with the infuser I got him. No more bothering with tea bags."

Zinnia reaches for the back of the patio chair as her mind spins. She'd never considered that Mother might unearth the truth, much less anticipated any attempt at revenge. Too late now; all too late.

"I know you think I'm foolish," Mother says, "but I see you. I see the whole garden from our bed, even early in the morning when you think I'm still asleep." She stands and nods toward the house behind her. "Arthur put in that bay window because he loved how I loved his flowers, how I appreciated them, even if I didn't know all the Latin names."

Her voice grows colder. "You, your arrogance, your judgment—you are your father's daughter in many ways, Zinnia, but *that* was never your father." She looks out beyond the tall back fence, into the canyon abutting the garden's edge. "He must have asked you to help him die, probably told you to keep me out of it. I wouldn't have been able to stop you, but the least you owe me now is to listen."

Zinnia can do nothing but stare and reel, her hands gripping the chair's back. She doesn't recognize the person in front of her. Every certainty she'd clung to so closely is slipping away, and there's nothing she can do.

"Sit." Mother reaches for her wrist. "It's temporary. You'll be fine by tomorrow."

Zinnia's legs begin to buckle, but Mother catches her. "I'll get you some tea to help with the swelling," Mother says as she guides Zinnia into the chair.

"Well, the hens have certainly come home to roost," Mother says as she pushes Zinnia toward the table. "Or is it chickens?" She smiles, her eyes narrowing playfully. "You can't even correct me this time, early worm," she says.

Zinnia can't help but smirk at the wry joke as Mother walks toward the sliding doors into the kitchen. She is bone tired: tired of fighting; tired of assembling each puzzle piece of thought into a tidy pattern; tired of herself and the weight she carries. When her mother returns with a steaming mug, she is too tired to resist the tears that come, or to push her mother's hand away when it clutches hers.

10

THE BLACK COAT

CORNELIA FEYE

The black coat waited in a booth in the Turkish Bazaar in Istanbul, long before Vega knew how much she needed it. It hung amidst soft leather bags, pungent spices, flowing silks, and customers speaking as many tongues as in the times of the Silk Road. It took a long and adventurous journey to find it there.

In the meantime Vega was far from exotic Istanbul stuck in a small German town on a gray winter afternoon. The phone rang with urgency. A lengthy pause on the other end of the line answered her greeting.

"I was trying to reach Vega?" said a male voice in a strong middle-eastern accent.

"Speaking."

"Can you drive to Tehran the day after tomorrow?" the voice asked abruptly.

Now Vega paused, considering that Tehran was five thousand kilometers away and that the proposition gave her little notice.

"What do you mean, drive to Tehran?" she asked lamely.

"I mean exactly what I said," the voice repeated, slightly impatiently. "Can you, or can you not drive a Mercedes Benz car to Tehran the day after tomorrow?" It began to dawn on her what he was after.

"You mean deliver a new Mercedes from the factory in Sindelfingen to Persia?" she tried to clarify.

"Of course. We leave in two days and we get to Tehran in a week. You deliver the car, we pay your way back to Germany plus five hundred Marks and you can be home by Christmas. Your friend Andy has driven cars for us before and he recommended you. He is not able to do it this time."

Vega remembered Andy telling her about his trips to Tehran. They had sounded exotic and exciting. The adventure was hers for the taking, plus the opportunity to earn spending money for Christmas, but suddenly she was not so sure any more.

"You drive in a caravan, don't you?" Vega asked, trying to show that she was not completely clueless. The man on the other end sighed.

"Yes, we drive with five cars in a caravan. My partner, Mordejai, and I are in the first and last car, and three German drivers are in the middle."

"Wouldn't it be easier to just put them on a car transporter?"

Another sigh of exasperation on the other end of the line. "Easier maybe, but also a lot more expensive. I told them that it was not a good idea to bring a woman along, but we don't have much time left and we ran out of options."

What a vote of confidence, Vega thought; she was their last choice, since they absolutely could not find anybody else.

"Do I have a bit of time to think about this? I have to make some arrangements before I can leave on such short notice."

"We don't have much time. As I said, we leave the day after tomorrow. The cars must be delivered by next week. Let me know by tomorrow morning at the latest." He gave her his number and hung up.

Two days later Vega sat in a brand new Mercedes Benz 450 S heading southeast on the Autobahn. Her adrenaline ran high, her seat was comfortable, and the radio played soft rock. She thought the elegant cream color of the Mercedes matched her khaki pants and the small leather bag containing the few pieces of clothing she had thrown together. She was on her way to a real adventure.

The idyllic drive through Austria, past green hills and picturesque villages on the well-maintained Autobahn, abruptly ended as they entered Yugoslavia. The Autobahn turned into a winding two-lane road. The Mercedes caravan shared the road with dilapidated local cars and dirt-splattered trucks transporting goods from Western to Eastern Europe. Vega's car was sandwiched in the middle of their caravan between Mustafa's Mercedes in the front, followed by Gerd, one of the German drivers. Behind her drove Mathew and Mordejai. If any driver had to stop or needed to go to the bathroom, he or she signaled with their high beams and the whole caravan came to a halt. Vega had to use the bathroom most frequently, which quickly resulted in grumbling by the rest of the all-male crew.

By the time they reached the Bulgarian border, the Mercedes didn't look so shiny anymore. Instead, it blended in nicely with the mud-encrusted trucks, and the driver's appearance started to match the car's in ruggedness and grime. Mustafa had omitted to mention that in order to drive five thousand kilometers in five days, they had no time to stop and sleep. This meant pulling over once in a while and napping on the back seat of the car for a few hours before continuing. As the roads got worse and worse, the mud got deeper and deeper and slowed down their traveling speed.

When they reached the border between Bulgaria and Turkey, Vega's eyes had black circles, her clothes were crinkled from wearing them for three days and nights, and she smoked nonstop to stay awake. Fortunately, there was no shortage of cigarettes. Mordejai had packed the trunk of his car with cigarette cartons and bottles of Chivas Regal whiskey. When Vega first saw this bounty, she was surprised at the limited choice of their supplies, especially since staples such as water bottles or simple food items were completely missing, but at the Turkish frontier, the wisdom of the selection became obvious: The border consisted of a large dirt field, crammed with trucks from all the Western European countries, trying to make their way into Asia. The truck drivers sat and waited in enormous lines that did not seem to move at all. Mordejai and their caravan, however, speedily drove to the front of the queue, past the waiting trucks. They crossed the border with the help of several bottles of Chivas and cigarette cartons, which disappeared quickly in the bags of smiling border guards. Vega was relieved that they did not have to drink all that whiskey themselves.

Vega celebrated crossing the bridge over the Bosporus in Istanbul, which links Europe and Asia, by turning up her radio full volume to a Turkish station playing Arabic songs. For the first time in her life she had reached the border of Europe and entered the continent of Asia. There was no time to stop or take pictures, but Vega now felt like a true adventurer. To make the celebration complete, they actually stayed at a hotel that night, and she got to change her clothes, take a shower, and sleep in a real bed with her legs stretched out. They had reached the halfway point of their journey. Little did she know that the worst was still to come.

After their caravan passed the Turkish capital, Ankara, and entered Eastern Turkey, the roads and the weather deteriorated. It was December after all. Erzurum, in the foothills of the Eastern Taurus Mountains, looked like Vega imagined a Siberian prison camp: gray, concrete-block buildings in the midst of a desolate landscape. After Erzurum, civilization ended. Dwellings, dug into the ground, and meager smoke columns, rising out of holes on the side of the road, were the only traces of human habitation. People lived in these earth holes, trying to stay warm underneath the frozen tundra. Vega felt sympathetic to them. Staying warm was not easy for her either, especially at nights, when they took their breaks. The men were able to go into chai shops along the road and drink tea. But as a woman, especially one without a head scarf, she would have been stoned on the spot if she had left her car, as Mustafa assured her. Mordejai and Mathew took pity on her and brought small glass cups of hot mint tea to her car, where she sat shivering in the night. She could have used a warmer coat.

Day number four almost marked the end of their journey. Mustafa hit a sheep that was crossing the road and the local villagers were ready to stone the whole caravan. Actually, several midsize pebbles hit Mustafa's windshield. Lengthy negotiations ensued. Vega was stranded in her car, since Mustafa had threatened to leave her behind if she dared to get out and show her face to the locals. Vega started to question the wisdom of undertaking this journey. Why on earth had she agreed to this ordeal? But then Gerd and Mathew joined her, and together they observed and commented the proceedings outside like an anthropological movie. Vega's windshield served as a screen, and they supplied their own soundtrack:

A dead sheep lies by the roadside. Two older, male villagers angrily berate a young, dark-haired Persian driver with a mustache and an arrogant expression. Several other villagers stand close by, stones in their fists. Another Persian man, slighter in build, tries to calm down the situation with soothing hand gestures. He opens the trunk of his tan Mercedes and takes out two bottles of Chivas Whiskey in golden gift boxes. He hands one to each of the elders. Next a carton of Marlboro cigarettes emerges from the trunk. The man gives the cigarette packages to the other villagers in attendance. Several hours pass.

It was getting dark by the time they resumed driving, and they still had to cross the Mount Ararat pass on their way to the Iranian border. Vega felt exhausted. A thin layer of ice hid underneath the dirt of the road. Vega's Mercedes suddenly started to slither. On her left, she saw the gaping abyss of the mountain cliff, on the right rocky outcroppings barred her way. The tires of her Mercedes lost traction and slid across the narrow road. In a terrifying moment, she had no control of the heavy car. *This is it*, Vega thought. My short life will end on the flanks of Mount Ararat, where Noah's ark once landed.

Fortunately this dramatic ending was not her fate. She applied the brakes and managed to steer the large vehicle as slowly as possible back onto the road. When she regained control of the car and pulled over at the first available turnout, her knees were shaking. Mustafa stopped his car and walked over. She lowered her window and was just about to assure him that she was all right, when he started to yell:

"I knew we should not have hired you. It was a bad idea from the start. Women can't drive; I knew that all along. Why did I ever even consider bringing you along? You are nothing but trouble from beginning to end. Do you realize you almost wrecked this valuable car? Do you even know that you cannot use your brakes on icy surfaces? How did you ever pass your driving test?"

Vega did not know what to say, so she just looked at him and did the worst thing under the circumstances: she started to cry.

The border crossing into Persia the next morning was no problem at all. Nobody was there. However, the reason for the deserted border presented a problem. The Iranian people had forced the Shah of Iran to leave the country. They expected their new leader, Ayatollah Khomeini, to arrive back from exile any day. The caravan of brand new Mercedes Benz limousines basically entered a country in the middle of a revolution. In a considerate gesture, their Iranian employers placed armed guards in three of the five Mercedes cars, including Vega's. The public mood was not in favor of foreign luxury cars being imported to rich Shah supporters in Tehran. Having a dark and brooding Iranian guard sitting next to her in the passenger seat, holding a loaded pistol on his lap, did not make Vega feel safer. The fact that they had no language in common and could not communicate did not improve her comfort level either. Feeling very vulnerable, she wished for a different kind of protection—body armor for example. She had wanted an adventure, and she certainly got one.

When they reached the Iranian capital of Tehran, a million

protesters, celebrating the departure of the hated Shah, clogged the streets. As an angry mob of protesters crowded around her car, banging on the windows with their fists, she again questioned the wisdom of accepting this driving job. Scared and tired, they navigated through the excited crowds with their now dilapidated caravan. With great relief they arrived at Mordejai's house, where they planned to recover for the next few days.

Mordejai's family welcomed Gerd and Vega warmly. Mathew went to Mustafa's house, and Vega hoped that she would never have to see Mustafa again. Their closest ally in Mordejai's household was a deaf and mute housekeeper. With her there was no language barrier. She kept cooking fried eggs for the pale visitors, because she assumed that was their favorite food. Vega and Gerd had to perform a complex pantomime to communicate that they would actually like to try some Persian cuisine.

After three days Gerd and Vega left the chaos of Tehran behind and took a bus back to Istanbul. They visited the Hagia Sophia and a Turkish bath and took a stroll through the famous Grand Bazaar. In an onslaught for the senses, miles of colorful stalls lined the covered market, offering everything from exotic spices to brocaded scarves in a seductive abundance of colors and textures. The traders and their wares seemed to have sprung forth from *The Tale of 1,001 Nights*. Turkish music blared, and samples of honey-sweet baklavas filled with ground pistachios teased their taste buds. Soft silk in rainbow colors from China flowed through their fingers, and the scent of orange cumin, displayed in big barrels, smelled as pungent as perfume. Vega was drawn to a stall with leather goods. There, like an apparition, the black coat waited for her in shiny splendor. She wanted this coat. She needed it. It was the answer to her prayers, providing warmth, protection, and power. The owner agreed to tailor-make a long, black leather coat to her exact measurements overnight.

When she picked it up the next day, it fit like a glove and cost almost her entire earnings for driving the Mercedes across Eastern Europe. It seemed well worth it. Overnight the tailor had created the most beautiful object she had ever possessed. In it Vega walked through the cold and drizzle of wintry Istanbul feeling like a conqueror. Forgotten were the tears, doubts, and fears from the flanks of Mount Ararat.

Vega decided to never take it off again. She pretty much kept her promise until two weeks later at a Christmas party back in Germany, where she left the coat in the wardrobe. Two hours later it was gone. The most perfect piece of clothing turned out to be the most impermanent as well. Vega thought that she had gone through a lot of hardship for such a short-lived reward.

She never found out who took the black leather coat, but she kept thinking about it. Two years later she went back to Istanbul and bought another coat at the exact same stall in the Turkish bazaar. The coat seemed to give her power when she wore it. Vega felt invincible, and when its long coattails flapped behind her, she could sweep all insignificant and petty concerns aside and be her most regal and confident self.

The second black leather coat unfortunately lasted only a couple of months. The circumstances of its loss were even more devastating than the first. Vega left it in her car one night, in a neighborhood she should have avoided, where she spent the night with a man she should have stayed away from. The next morning, the car windows were broken and the coat was gone.

She felt the universe was sending her a message. Maybe this was her punishment for being careless. Maybe she should not have spent the night at this location. Maybe this coat was not for her. Maybe she was not ready for the coat. Maybe she was not tough enough or was too frivolous and vain. Maybe she was getting too attached to the coat; maybe a floor length black leather coat was not the appropriate attire for a peace-loving aspiring Buddhist. Maybe it made her more aggressive and cocky than was good for her. Maybe someone else needed the coat more than she. Whatever the message, Vega received it loud and clear: *NO MORE LONG BLACK LEATHER COATS!*

She started wearing cotton. It felt less powerful, but none of her jackets disappeared. Eventually she stopped thinking about the black coat. But when she watched the *Matrix,* she admired Neo, Morpheus, and Trinity striding toward their next confrontation with Agent Smith in their long black coats, looking cool, in control, and invincible. Vega knew exactly how they felt.

Years later, the coat walked into Vega's office. A Russian woman with a big heart wore it. Trying not to sound overly excited, Vega said casually, "Luda, that's a great coat."

"You like it?" Luda answered enthusiastically in her thick Russian accent.

"Yes, it is very cool!"

"It makes me feel so powerful," she exclaimed. Vega allowed herself a little smile, remembering what it felt like.

"My husband brought it back from Turkey for me. It is a great coat, but I wish I could wear it more often. Mostly it is too hot here," she continued.

"I once had a coat like this." Vega said quietly.

"Really? When you lived in Germany? What happened to it?" Luda asked.

"I lost it, twice."

"You want to try it on? You should try it on!" She took off the coat, and Vega slipped into it.

"It fits you perfectly. You should have this coat. I'll give it to you. I barely wear it." Luda poured out this generous offer.

"Oh, no. It's yours. You look great in it. Thanks for letting me try it on." Vega quickly took off the coat and handed it back to her.

"But it is perfect for you. It looks like it belongs to you. How did you lose your coat?"

"It was a long time ago. It got stolen. Actually, two identical coats got stolen."

"Two? I have two coats like this. My husband brought one for me and one for my daughter. But she never wears it and does not like it."

"Thanks, that is very generous of you, but I cannot accept it."

"Of course you can. It is meant to be. One coat just hangs in my closet. It was waiting for you."

Despite Vega's protests a brand-new, black leather coat waited for her in her office a few days later. She picked it up gingerly. This coat had come to her; she didn't have to make an arduous journey to get it. She put it on. It fit like a second skin, like armor. Walking out onto the street she felt invincible again.

Suddenly a car hit the brakes with screeching tires. It swerved in front of her, as Vega tried to sidestep it, but the car caught her left shoulder. She fell and skidded across the surface of the rough road like a sled on ice. She tumbled and turned as the car hit the curb. Vega came to a halt at the opposite curb, lifting her arm to shield her head from the impact. The impact came, but it was muffled. Vega moaned, lying on her side. Her hip hurt like crazy. She heard voices, shouting, screams, a siren approaching; she just wanted to lie there huddled in her leather coat. The coat was ripped; the abrasions from the road surface had destroyed its shiny texture. There was a big hole in the sleeve.

But it had protected her, when she needed it most.

FUNERAL CALL

TAMARA MERRILL

It's 10 p.m. on the West Coast when the phone rings. I answer, expecting to hear that a friend has a problem. Instead a voice I don't recognize says, "Hi, this is Katrina."

I say, "Who?"

The voice responds, "Katrina."

I say, "Who?"

"Katrina."

I hang up.

The phone rings again.

"How the fuck many Katrinas do you know?"

It dawns on me. I know who this is—my sister. Cautiously I say, "Hey, Katrina." I knew it was important. No one in the family has called my number in twenty-two years, and unless things have changed she is three time zones away, making it 1 a.m. her time.

"Mother, wants to see you. Dad died yesterday, and she wants us all home for the funeral."

"I don't think that's a good idea."

"Mother said to call."

Yep, I thought, *and you're still doing whatever she wants.* "No way, I'm busy."

"Would it kill you to be nice? You don't even know when it is."

Oh yeah. I've heard that a few too many times in my life—amazing how the kid-triggers still work; I fall back into my old childhood habits and snarl, "I am being nice, believe me, you don't want to know what I'm thinking."

"But, Tat, Mother asked me to call everyone and get them here."

"By everyone—what makes you think she means me, too? He wasn't my father."

"Well, I guess she didn't really mention your name, but she told me to call everyone."

"Listen," I say carefully, "you better check with her. I doubt that she wants me anywhere near that funeral. And, how did you get this number anyway?"

"It was in mother's phone book."

What? How is that possible? I've moved several times in the twenty years since my mother basically kicked me out of the family and cut me off from my siblings—my half-siblings. Had that old witch been keeping track of me all this time? Keeping track, watching, judging, making sure I stayed far away.

I refuse again and get off the phone. I put on my pajamas and try to read but the call won't leave me alone.

You probably can guess that I come from a dysfunctional family, as they say in the books, but if you ask my family they will tell you that I'm the only dysfunctional one and that without my disruptions life is better for all of them. And maybe it is—no contact means that I stopped checking up on "the family" a long time ago. Wiped them out of my mind, never did a Google search on anyone.

I pour a glass of wine and reach for my laptop. Tonight a Google search sounds like a good idea.

I start with my mother—she's old, but she's famous in her field. I figure even if Google only returns recent history she'll be there. She is. Doesn't look too bad either for a seventy-five-year-old, I wonder if she had a face-lift. Probably more than one. Clicking around I find a picture of the family at some special event. Mother, Father, my four half-siblings, spouses, and kids galore. Everyone looks pretty normal. I wonder how many were drunk—or perhaps this was taken before the fun started.

I spot a familiar face. *Is that my old boyfriend, Darrel, in the back? Must be. He's bald!* Wow! I could probably pass these people on the street and wouldn't know them. But then they wouldn't know me either, and I prefer to keep it that way. I pick out my sisters, Sue and Katrina, and my bothers, Mike and Hank. I can't tell who is married to whom or which kids belong to which.

I find an interview someone did with my mother when her last book came out. Pretty good. Six best sellers, all in her field. Parenting! I've seen a couple in the Barnes & Noble window, but I've never read one—nor admitted the author was my mother. I know way too much about her parenting skills from firsthand knowledge. I skim through the interview. *Well, look at that, surprise, surprise—she only mentions raising four children.* Guess that's not really a lie, even though there are five of us. In all this time I'm sure she's put me completely out of her mind.

I changed the search to my old boyfriend Darrel's name. He pops right up. Still married to my sister Sue—half-sister, actually. Their little indiscretion during my freshmen year of college—when Darrel and I had been dating—appears to have led to a child. The birthdate is only six months after he dumped me. *Lucky Sue—wonder if he's still a cheater.* He looks like one even with the bald head. He seems to have made a lot of money. Sue would like that. She looks like I remember mother looking when I was a kid, but that dyed hair could use a root touch up. *Bet she hates this picture.*

Next I Google my older sister, Katrina. *Wow! Lots of degrees. Never married.* That surprises me. She used to always have a doll tucked into her arms when we were kids. Maybe being the oldest taught her she didn't really want any of her own. *Wait two kids—what? Wonder what mother had to say about that? Hmm—the father is some French guy—so it's probably okay.* With mother anything French was always better than anything American. *Nice beach house; must have a good job.* I check LinkedIn. Can't find her. Back to Google. She's still tall and thin —looks good. Can't find a picture of the French guy. But her son is a basketball star at ASU.

Mike, the second child, isn't as easy to find—all I get is a couple of references to him as mother's kid and Katrina's brother. He seems to be living off the grid. Wonder what he's been doing for twenty years. Probably drugs—that was what he was doing last time I saw him. Of course, that was twenty-two years ago and people change. I certainly have.

I'm the third child. I don't need to look up myself. I already know that there are no links between me and my family on Google. I keep an eye on my own name. I don't actually want people to know about me anymore than my mother does. I was born of a "one-night mistake" my mother made. This makes me the child with no father. The one who always knew she had no father—the one who didn't act or look like the others. That's me!

I was very young when I figured out I was adopted and therefore not quite as good as the rest of the kids in my family. But it wasn't until I was thirteen that my "father" let it slip in a fit of anger that I wasn't really adopted. I was my mother's "indiscretion" and her "bastard," which is technically true since my mother wasn't married to my father. She was, of course, married to the man who is on my birth certificate, the father of the other four. I hadn't been adopted because it wasn't necessary—however—he made sure to tell me again and again that I wasn't his child, that I had no father.

I Google back to mother—scanning the pictures to find Mike— he's in a few but not many, and now that I take a good look—only the recent ones. Maybe he hid for a while, too. When we were kids, hiding was our specialty—even if we knew the consequences—it always seemed better to hide as long as possible—and sometimes— not often—it even worked. Guess if mother has my address and numbers in her book I haven't been hiding very successfully.

I Google search for the baby of the family, Hank. He hated his name—Henri. It's one thing for girls to have "fancy" names—Katrina,

Suzette, Tatiana—but with boys it's different. There was no way to make Henri a good Midwestern name except to call him Hank. For some perverse reason mother refused to allow us to do that at home —insisting that we always use his "proper name."

I actually find him as Henri (Hank) Kimble. Maybe he grew into the name. *He's a psychiatrist! Guess that makes sense.* Lives in Florida with a beautiful family. *Damn—never would have guessed he'd turn out so well. He was such a weird kid.*

Perhaps, I really am the only dysfunctional one—well, maybe Mike and I. Two out of five, 40%; not that good for a "parenting expert." I go back to the interview with my mother—she talks about four children, but I can only find reference by name to the two successful ones.

I realize I'm being petty, but it feels pretty good to let it flow. I may think I haven't thought about this family junk in years but it's never far from the surface—I've just become really good at stopping the thoughts when they come.

I skim the stuff about my mother's husband, how supportive of her career, what a good father to his children—nicely said—his children, maybe, but not to me. Of course, there is no mention of the middle child, me. Well, of course there isn't. But just so you know, if parents are going to act like all the children belong to the family in public, they really should act like it at home, too. It was very confusing to me, as a child, when my parents told obvious lies. Enough. I close the computer and tell myself to stop thinking.

It's 6:05 a.m.; the shrill ring of my phone drags me out of a deep sleep. *Damn.* I knew it was Katrina but I answered anyway. "Yah?"

"Good Morning, Tat."

I grunt.

"We all think you should come."

"No thanks. This isn't a good time for a reunion." *Maybe when the old witch dies but not now.* I keep that thought to myself.

"Oh, Tat." I hear Katrina's deep exasperated, sigh. "Please? Mother really wants to see you."

I refuse again and hang up, but now, of course, I can't sleep. I get in the shower. I hear the phone. There is no way in hell I'm getting out to answer. As I towel off I glance at the screen. I don't recognize the number. It's an area code I'm unfamiliar with, so it must be one of the others. I dress and make coffee, ignoring the persistent missed call message blinking on the screen.

I don't have to answer, but I can't stop thinking about the past. I came home from college at the end of my freshman year believing that Darrel and I were a couple and that he was my ally in the war with my mother. Instead, he and my sister Sue arrived together for our date and told me they were a couple. Naturally, I didn't handle it well. Darrel had never mentioned anything in our twice-weekly phone calls, and I was caught completely off guard.

I didn't exactly threaten them, but I was close to it and there were some nasty words exchanged. It ended with Sue telling me she never wanted to see me again and with mother suggesting it would be better if I moved out. So I did. I went back to the city where I was attending college, bunked with a friend who had an apartment and no roommate. By the end of the summer I had a job that allowed me to rent a room of my own while I finished my education. My freedom from the family was surprisingly exhilarating.

At first I'd get an occasional phone call, but it was easy to drift from the family and by the time I graduated I had no contact with anyone. Over the years I became an expert at evading questions from friends or colleagues about my family. I gradually stopped thinking about them and simply moved on.

Now, all this time later, they want back in. I'm not ready for that. When I'd been married, Tim had always wanted to talk about my childhood. It was easier for me to divorce him than it was to explain. Luckily we'd had no children.

I have a great job and a full circle of friends. We don't pry into each other's pasts. I live by the credo that now is what's important and anything that happened before thirty is irrelevant. I finish my coffee and go to work.

By afternoon, I've let it all go. When my desk phone rings, I pick it up without hesitation. This time I recognize the voice at once. "Hey, Mike." I smile into the phone. This is the brother who was my champion. When mother would put me in the closet to "cool off," he'd lie on the floor and whisper to me through the crack under the door. I'd actually like to know how his life is going.

"Kat called and gave me your number. Hope it's alright to call you at work." He sounds cautious.

I guess I shouldn't be surprised that mother knew where I worked, but I am. "It's fine, Mike. I'm just a little stunned to hear your voice." He chuckles and I laugh a little myself. "So," I continue, "Are you going to the big funeral?"

"I'm already here. Please come. I know you don't really want to see Mother, but she's mellowed and with Dad gone ..." Mike doesn't finish his thought.

"Mellowed?" I sneer and repeat the word. "I don't remember anything mellow about her, ever."

"She's getting old, and maybe with Dad dying she realizes she won't live forever. I think she wants to clean up her mistakes, make amends."

Anything is possible I suppose. "So are you a shrink now, too? You sound like one."

Mike laughs a real laugh this time. "Nah," he tells me, "just many years of rehab." I smile and click my pen a few times. I realize I would like to see this brother.

"How are the others?" I ask. Mike and I always called them "the others"; us against them.

"Same, just older. Sue is a prig. Katrina is perfect, and I'm the "drug addict." You're the "bad girl." This time I really laugh and he joins me.

"Why don't you just fly out here to see me?" I ask. "We'll have a lovely weekend together and catch up. It would be more fun. Less drama and no dead bodies."

He's quiet for a long minute before he answers. "That's sounds great, Tat, but I don't run away anymore."

Now it's my turn to be silent. Finally I admit, "I don't think I can face the family. I've built this whole life without them."

"I'll be here," he says very quietly. "I've got your back."

I know he does. I remember how he tried to protect me. We talk a few more minutes, and I promise to think about it. My hands are shaking as I hang up the phone. I wonder what else my mother knows about my life and what she's told everyone.

After work and my second glass of wine I get up the nerve to go. I quickly buy nonrefundable tickets on the Internet and write a hasty email to work telling them I'll be out for a few days. The Dutch courage I found in my wine abandons me, and I toss and turn all night. I don't call to tell anyone in the family that I'm coming.

I change planes in Denver and settle down in my aisle seat with the latest Jodi Picoult novel. I try not to make eye contact with anyone coming on board. As the plane jolts down in Minneapolis, I come awake. Thanks to my sleepless night I've snoozed away the entire flight. I change my watch and realize that I'll have to hurry to get to Patterson's for the viewing.

When we were kids, Mike and I used to ride our bikes downtown and try to peak into their windows in the hopes that we'd see a dead body. We never did. My stomach is in the same kind of anticipation knot I used to feel then. *This probably isn't a good idea. I should just turn around. Change my ticket and head home.* I trudge to the rental car line.

It's freezing here. My Southern California coat and boots are no match for the ice and snow that fill the funeral home parking lot. I run my fingers through my hair. Check my lipstick and push open the door. The old house is just as creepy as it was when we buried my grandmother. I read the board, find my "father's" name, and head for the Lilac Room.

Wow. I'm surprised by the crowd. It looks like any other party except, of course, for the pale pink coffin at the front of the large room. *Pale pink? Weird choice.*

For a moment no one notices me. Then Mike shouts my name, hurries across the room, picks me up, and whirls me around. As I hug him tight, the room falls deadly silent.

"Tatiana." I'd know that steely tone anywhere. Mother approaches looking regal and, I have to admit it, way younger than she should. I have time to think, *Great facelift*, before she says, "Michael put your sister down. Try to remember where you are."

"Hello, Mother," I say. Mike puts me down but keeps his arm around my shoulders. Mother and I don't touch.

"We'll talk later," she says and turns back to her guests.

Mike grins. "We're in trouble now," he says.

I make a face. "What else is new?"

The buzz in the room picks up, and I can feel everyone looking at me. Sue and Katrina appear. I manage to respond to their hugs. It would look strange to the guests if I didn't. I came to this thing, so I need to make the best of it. We exchange casual chitchat, like the strangers we are. I meet Sue's daughter. She looks just like Darrel, but she seems nice enough.

Katrina reminds Sue that they need to mingle, and they move off. Mother is drinking a glass of champagne, and I can see her watching our every move as she accepts condolences from a bunch of people I don't recognize.

"Champagne?" I ask Mike.

He shrugs. "Mother wanted it. Patterson said he'd never heard of such a thing but ..." we finish together "what Mother wants, Mother gets." We laugh and Mother frowns in our direction. I pretend not to notice.

An elderly woman approaches and scrutinizes me. "So, you're the troublemaker that moved to California." She's not asking. She's simply telling me, but I nod. "Your poor mother." She shakes her head at me and walks off.

"Who was that?" I ask Mike.

"Lilah Erickson."

"Lilah? As in mother's friend Lilah? She looks so old."

"Twenty years is a long time. I think we've all changed."

I look across the room, "Not mother."

"That would be the skillful work of a good surgeon, a strict diet, and as she would tell you a disciplined life."

"Oh yes, the disciplined life, I remember those lectures."

Mike hugs me. "Let's get you a glass of bubbly. I think you're going to need it."

Mike stays close and whispers names to me when people approach and offer condolences. I barely speak to any of them. I feel no sorrow over the death of the man in the coffin. It seems wrong to pretend I do. I know that these strangers speak to me because they want to get a good look at the "evil woman" from California. I'm glad I'm wearing a kick-ass designer suit and amazing boots. No one asks anything personal. I'm just a carny sideshow. I can see them whisper to each other and look in my direction. Why did I come?

The crowd thins. The lights dim. Katrina seems to be in charge of herding the last few out the door. I excuse myself and head for ladies room. I'm here, but I'm still not ready to face Mother.

Sue blocks my way. "Hey, Tat. Where're you going?"

"I'll be right back."

"Can it wait? Mother wants a word with all of us."

I shrug and turn back into the room.

Mother stands in front of the coffin flanked by Katrina and Hank. Sue glides over and joins them, leaving Mike and me to stand facing the group. I almost shudder, but I catch myself. I learned a long time ago not to show weakness even when I feel trapped, and I do feel trapped. Katrina winks at me. What? I didn't expect that.

"Let's go get some dinner, Mother. You can talk to us there." Katrina says breaking the spell that has been holding us all.

"Tatiana needs to say goodbye to her father before we go. The casket will be closed tomorrow." Mother watches my face as she speaks.

I stay serene. Inside I may still be fifteen, but outside I'm forty-two, calm and rational. "I'm good," I say and turn to the door. "Where are we headed?" I've got a rental; I can meet you there."

"Canton Road, of course. I'll ride with Tat." Mike grabs a jacket off the rack by the door, and we leave without looking at anyone.

I search my purse for the car keys. My hands are shaking. I pull out the keys and hand them to Mike. "You drive. I have no idea how to get to the restaurant, and I haven't driven on icy roads in years."

Mike takes the keys and opens the passenger door for me. I know he can see I'm upset, but he thankfully doesn't say anything. We drive a few miles in silence. I watch the lights and the buildings slide past the icy window.

I grew up in this city, but nothing looks familiar until I see the high school. Canton Road is in the next block. It was the only Chinese restaurant in town when I was growing up, and it has always been the place Mother takes us to be seen. We wore our best clothes and paid vigilant attention to our manners. We'd been carefully taught how to behave like a perfect family in public.

Mike parks next to a huge snowbank. Across the lot, Katrina and her children climb out of a large SUV. Katrina says something, and the kids laugh; the tall boy gives her a hug.

Mike smiles in their direction. "Katrina is a great mom." I can hear the unspoken subtext—*unlike our mother*. We watch them cross the lot and enter the restaurant before we get out of the car.

"What about the others?" I ask. He shrugs, and I take that to mean he doesn't want to talk about it. This is going to be a long couple of days.

Mike takes my hand and swings it. "Come on. Let's get this done."

I square my shoulders, and he pulls open the carved restaurant door. Memories assault me from every direction. It smells the same. It looks the same. I think the old women at the hostess desk may be the same. The others are gathered at the big round table in the corner, the one with the lazy Susan in the middle, the one we always sat at. Mother watches us approach. Mike squeezes my hand before he lets go. Katrina smiles at me. I feel protected.

A round of drinks appears. Everyone has switched to the "hard stuff." I order a vodka tonic. Mike asks for a Diet Coke. Mother gives him one of those looks. "Oh for heaven's sake, Michael, your father just died. Order a drink. One certainly won't hurt you."

"Actually, Mother, it would."

I'm impressed by how calmly he responds. Mother shakes her head and purses her lips. Another look I remember all too well. This one means *Don't be ridiculous*, but Mike just ignores her. She lifts her glass and turns to me. "I'd offer a toast to the return of the prodigal daughter, but since I understand that you had to be dragged here, I don't think that would be appropriate."

I feel her anger, but I'm determined to follow Mike's lead. If he can act like a grown up, so can I.

Katrina lifts her glass. "I think a toast to Tat is a great idea." Mother turns her icy glare on her.

She doesn't seem to notice. Instead Katrina tilts her glass in my direction and says, "To the one that got away."

Mike instantly lifts his glass and clicks it against Kat's. All seven grandchildren join the toast. Hank clinks his glass with mine and even says, "To Tat." Sue and Darrel don't move. The battle lines have been drawn.

"Don't you think a toast to our father's memory would be more suitable?" Sue asks Katrina.

"No, I don't." Katrina doesn't back down or flinch. "I am delighted to see Tat. I think it has been much too long since she was welcome here." She smiles innocently at Sue and then at mother and continues as she lifts her glass again, "To Father."

We, all, obediently raise our glasses and chorus, "To Father."

Mother has always ruled us with an iron hand. She is strong willed and completely sure of herself. This is the first time I've ever seen a crack in that control. I watch Kat as she talks to the family. She seems at ease. Sue, on the other hand, is tense. I can see how tightly she is grasping the fork she is tapping against the table. Mother frowns at Sue, and the tapping stops but she doesn't uncurl her fist.

The waiter approaches, and Mother asks Sue to order for all of us and reminds her to order that "awful sweet and sour pork" that Tatiana likes. I smile what I hope is a nice smile and say, "Actually, I'm a vegetarian."

"Oh for heaven's sake, Tatiana, don't be pretentious. We all know you live in California. That doesn't mean you're vegetarian."

Crap. My brain seizes for a moment, and then I look at Kat. She's actually laughing. Is that good or bad? All the old family dynamics are rushing in, and I want to run. I remind myself that I am Tatiana Kaufman. I am forty-two years old. I hold a master's in business administration. I have a prestigious job and am considered an expert in my field. I do not need to feel intimidated by anyone. Mike squeezes my hand, and I lift my head and look straight at Mother for the first time. I speak in a level, well-modulated voice, "Actually, none of you know anything about me."

"And whose fault is that?" The cold fire in mother's eyes would have caused me to burst into tears and run from the room when I was here last, but now I find myself growing calm.

The knot in my stomach releases for the first time. "Yours, Mother," I answer careful to keep all accusation out of my voice. Mother's eyes widen and her nostrils flare. Despite my childhood training I refuse to feel fear. "I left your house in anger and I never contacted you, but it seems that you've always known exactly where I live and yet I've never heard from you and"—I make a wild guess—"you never let anyone else contact me either."

Katrina turns toward Mother. She takes a deep breath and talks to me as she keeps her eyes focused on Mother. "She told us you had to be committed, Tat. She said you had a breakdown caused by drug abuse, that you'd tried to kill yourself and that your doctors didn't want any of us to interfere with your treatment."

I stare at Katrina and then look at Mike. I'm shocked. Speechless. Slowly I look at the others. Hank is watching Mother. He looks as shocked as I feel. Sue tosses her hair defiantly and defends Mother. "Last time I saw you, you were certainly acting crazy. If you weren't committed you should have been."

"Twenty-two years." I can't quite take it in. I look at Mike and ask, "You thought I was crazy for twenty-two years?"

He twists his napkin and looks directly at me, embarrassed but unashamed. "I've only been sober two years, Tat. I didn't think of anything but drugs and alcohol for a long time." He reaches for my hand, but I pull back. "When I got straight I asked about you but Mother told me you didn't want to have contact with any of us and I accepted that."

Kat leans forward, and her son touches her arm in support. I'm seeing everything in slow motion. My head is swimming. I miss the first few words of Kat's excuse: "... after I came back from France, Mother's story just didn't make sense. I tried to find you, but now I know I was looking in all the wrong places. You've never been hospitalized have you?"

I shake my head. "I never even disappeared until after graduation." I look at Mother and continue. "I was angry when Mother threw me out." She starts to protest, but I raise my hand and she stops and looks away. Sue takes her hand and holds it. "I took a room and got a job and when I graduated from college I sent Mother an announcement. But, I guess, she never mentioned that."

"How could you do this, Mother?" Hank asks. He turns to me and tears are running down his cheeks. "She told me you'd tried to take your own life, that you'd tried to harm Sue and that she'd had no choice but to have you hospitalized. When I didn't stop asking to go see you she said you'd found a way to kill yourself."

Hank continues, carefully articulating each word. "I became a psychiatrist because I wanted to stop others from killing themselves. Until Kat said you would come to this funeral, I thought you were dead." He looks around the table, studying each face. "Why didn't any of you tell me?"

The waiter approaches the table but he senses the tension and backs away quickly, leaving us to our confrontation. I need to understand this. I clench my fist under the table and keep my voice level as I address mother. "How could you tell my siblings that I was crazy." Tears fill my eyes, but I force them away. I will not let her see me cry. "How could you say I was dead?"

"You were dead, dead to me." Mother speaks these words in her professional voice and I cringe. That tone was always followed by punishment that was "for your own good." "When I asked Katrina to call the family it never occurred to me that she would call you, but, once it was done, I decided this would be as good a time as any for you to clear the air between us." She studies me carefully. Mike squeezes my hand. Sue looks at me like she's seeing something slimy crawl out from under a rock. Katrina looks at the table. When I don't respond, Mother finishes her thought, "I believe you owe me an apology, Tatiana."

Did I hear that right? An apology for what? Katrina slams her chair back from the table. Her son catches it before it can topple over. If steam could actually come out of someone's ears it would be happening now, to Katrina. She glares at Mother and then includes Sue in her contemptuous gaze. "That's enough of this ridiculous behavior. If anyone is owed an apology it is Tatiana." She turns to me and tentatively holds out her hand. I take it. "Tat, I don't know how or why I continued to believe Mother when she told us that we should leave you alone, that you didn't want contact with any of us. I should have known better, and I am so sorry." She squares her shoulders, and, still holding my hand, she looks back to mother. "Whatever game you are playing, Mother, it won't work this time."

"Katrina," Mother says calmly, "I know you're upset about your father's death but I really can't allow you to talk to me in that tone." Sue pats the back of mother's hand and nods in agreement.

"I am upset," Katrina agrees. "Upset by your duplicitous behavior.

What possible good could it to do to deliberately separate one of your children from her family?"

Sue hisses, "Sit down and shut up. You're making a scene."

"Damn right, I am." Katrina is visibly shaking. "This family needs to face the truth. Mother is a bully, and we all let her do it." Sue's mouth falls open. Mother begins to shake her head no. But Katrina is on a roll. She continues, "You are, Mother. You're a very polite, very charming bully who tries to control everything about this family. We all do what you say because we're afraid of your wrath. Hank and I live far away from here so that we don't have to spend time with you. Mike struggles every day with an addiction that you pretend never existed. Sue has never grown up. And"—she takes a deep breath and looks at me before she continues—"you never liked Tatiana and we all knew it."

We sit in stunned silence. In our family we never, never, never talk back to Mother. Well, that's not true I talked back a lot, but look where that got me. Mother doesn't raise her voice. Instead she speaks very calmly, "That's quite enough, Katrina. I'm sure you don't want to say anything you will regret."

"I only regret not telling someone about how you and Dad treated Tatiana. Mike tried years ago, and I didn't back him up. I'm so sorry, Tat." She's crying freely now. I finally unfreeze, stand, and wrap my arms around my sister. Mike wraps his arms around us both. It feels great to be in the middle of their hug. Hank hurries around the table and joins us.

"Tatiana was a very troubled child. I tried to love her but it wasn't easy. Your father and I did the best we could in a very difficult situation." There is no remorse in mother's statement, just a sense of scientific explanation.

Words leap about in my head. I want to scream out. Defend myself against her depiction of me. Before I can say anything, Hank takes over.

"If in fact there was a difficult situation, it is one you created yourself, Mother. Tatiana was an innocent child trying to please adults who couldn't be satisfied. Kat is right. You've bullied and cajoled and manipulated us all. Why didn't you just leave your marriage when you found out you were pregnant?"

"I didn't want a divorce." Mother is unruffled. I've always known she was calculating, but this is more than that. This is self-preservation. "Your father and I loved each other very much. I was unfortunate enough to become impregnated by someone else. By the time your father and I realized that this child could not be his, it was too late to get an abortion."

I want to scream. I've told myself that I was a "love child," that I was the result of a tragic love affair, or that, perhaps, my birth father had died before I was born. After all this time I didn't think her words would hurt so much, but they do. Unwanted and unloved equals unworthy. *Stop*, I shout in my head. Over the years I've developed a coping technique that works for me—I just refuse to think about memories that hurt. I don't talk about them or "work through" them; I just don't allow myself to think about them. All the books (and I've read a lot) say to never "stuff" your emotions. But stuffing works, not in the middle of the night maybe, but in this situation it works. I'm still safely in the middle of the hug, and I manage to say calmly, "Thank you for being honest, Mother."

She huffs at me and takes a long drink from her cocktail, then turns to Sue and says, "I'm very tired and tomorrow is a long day. I'd like to leave now." Sue and Darrel leap to their feet and help mother into her coat. No one else moves. They leave dragging their reluctant daughter with them not saying another word to anyone.

Kat's sons are grinning. "Welcome home," the oldest one says to me.

The tension is broken, and we all laugh, order food, and talk about everything except Mother and the funeral. This will never be a "normal" family, but for the first time in a long time I feel like I have a family.

12

LAST MAGIC TRICK

CORNELIA FEYE

My father wanted to die in a tuxedo. He got his wish. He had always thought of himself as a glamorous performer and magician, and when I was a teenager he disappeared from my life. I was doing fine without him, living in a small university town studying art history—something he would never have approved. When he called me out of the blue, I was shocked.

"Why don't you ever call me? I haven't heard from you in ages," said his familiar and accusing voice.

"How did you get this number?" I asked.

"Your mother gave it to me. But seriously, why don't you talk to me?"

"I don't want to talk to you, because you remind me of what I hate about myself." There was a moment of silence at the other end of the line. Then, tentatively, he recovered.

"Okay, then let's meet and talk about that."

I had expected a tantrum, an insult, a slammed down receiver, but not this calm and conciliatory offer.

"How about getting together?" He wasn't giving up.

"Okay, let's meet on my turf." I didn't want to visit my father in the stifling apartment he shared with his second wife. She owned the apartment and there was no place to sit next to all the embroidered pillows and stuffed animals.

I suggested The Golden Trout, an old-fashioned, wood-paneled restaurant in the town center. It was more expensive than what I could afford. We would meet on neutral territory for lunch, nothing as intimate as dinner or as personal as my home.

When I entered the cozy dining room of The Golden Trout, my father already waited. He rose, all charm and chivalry, when he saw me. Unfortunately his gray beard, the vain smile, and the much too youthful denim leisure suit did not flatter him. I had seen him practice his smile in front of the mirror: a slight raise of the left eyebrow, coupled with a twinkle and a half-crooked lifting of one corner of his lips to achieve the desired effect of appearing cool and appraising at the same time. Apparently his charm had worked wonders on many women over the years, but it did not impress me. We ordered trout.

"So, what is it in me that reminds you of your own faults?" he asked, not wasting much time with small talk. I could have rattled off a long list: his false smile, vanity, self-righteousness, inflated ego, sense of self-importance, bad temper ... but I had to start with something simple.

"You pretend to be more than you really are. You are neither honest nor authentic."

That should give him something to chew on. My father pulled a trout bone from between his teeth and swallowed.

"How do you mean?" he asked. "Can you give an example?"

"You were an insurance clerk, all of my life, yet you always cultivated the magician role, and pretended you were an illusionist, when in fact you never even did any magic." I knew this would hurt, but he had asked for it.

"I had my own traveling magic show, with musicians and dancers. I was Harry Piper, the Mysterious. I showed you the programs—"

"That was forty years ago, after the war. It was over before you even met mom."

"I did a magic show at my fiftieth birthday party," he declared proudly.

"That was one day out of twenty-five years, in our living room in front of our family."

"I rejoined the Magic Circle," he announced. I sighed. This was not going anywhere. I knew the Magic Circle was the guild of professional magicians, and my father wanted to hold on to this part of his identity with tooth and nail. He could not see my point or understand that I was struggling hard to be true to myself.

"I am trying to be honest and real instead of creating an illusion," I said.

"I don't know what you are talking about. Being a magician is a profession; it's a calling."

"Okay, here is another example: you don't respect women," I said.

"This is very unfair; I love women, I worship them," he exclaimed emphatically.

"You love them as long as they admire you and as long as you are superior. But you don't respect them for who they are."

"What's that supposed to mean?" he snapped.

"You did it to Mom and me. You loved us as long as we were young, uncritical, and naïve. But when we became independent, and started to make our own money, and our own decisions, you felt threatened. You cheated on mom, divorced her, and married a woman even younger than her. You tried to stop me from going to college. You wanted me to become a mail carrier at the age of sixteen, because you said education was a waste for a woman, who gets married anyway."

"Well, it is—"

"What if I never get married? What if I am smart enough to make my own living?"

"You were always too smart for your own good," he sighed. I was used to this kind of remark. We were on familiar territory.

"Besides, how does my 'being disrespectful to women' remind you of the worst in yourself?" he asked slyly. He thought he had me cornered.

"I want to be taken seriously as a person, not just a pretty girl. I don't want to play the girly game you tried to teach me. When I wanted something, you used to say 'If you are nice to me and sit on my lap, you can have anything.'"

"What is so bad about that? And in the end you did what you wanted anyway."

"It was bad, because you didn't take me seriously.'

"You were always so rational and confrontational. Don't you know that you can achieve much more with female charm?"

"I don't want to achieve things with female charm. I want to be respected for what I know and who I am as a person, not just as a woman."

My father pushed his trout to the side. It was only half eaten. I used the opportunity to finish mine. It was delicious, much better than cafeteria food.

"That's the kind of ideas they put into your head at these universities," he mumbled. "What can I do? I am a self-made man!"

Now he was using his difficult childhood as an excuse to keep his family down and prevent us from having a better education than his. I knew he was an illegitimate child who grew up with his grandmother and went to school for merely eight years. I knew his early years had been hard, and he had to overcome many disadvantages, but why didn't he want his children to have a better life? I knew I was lucky to be able to go to university, something my father had not been able to do. The trout and a glass of cabernet had mellowed me. Maybe I just had substituted contempt with pity.

After lunch we walked down the cobblestone streets through the university town. The old Tudor houses leaned precariously over the narrow streets. Red geranium window boxes craned out like small balconies. It was the quiet hour after lunch. Students were either in class or taking a nap.

"How do you make ends meet? I mean what do you live on?"

"I get by. I have a scholarship and a job."

"What's your job?"

"I work three nights a week in a bar."

"Doing what?"

"I serve drinks. The owner of the bar is also my landlord."

"I'd like to see where you live."

"I live in an attic room of an old building not far from here."

"Can I come up?"

"Alright, but I only have an hour."

"How are you going to make a living when you're done with your studies? How do you think you can survive as an art historian?"

"What is it to you? I have never asked you for money, and I never will."

"I just don't understand why you waste your time studying something so impractical."

"I study what I love, and art is what keeps me going. I also take classes in ethnology."

"Well that's a relief," said my father in a rare sojourn into sarcasm.

"Here we are. Just to let you know, it is a fourth floor walk-up."

He had to stop and rest twice on the rickety, wooden stairs, huffing and puffing.

"Feeling my age," he said.

Feeling the cigarettes, I thought.

My attic room overlooked the steep gabled roofs of the town. I served tea. All his life my father had expected to be served by women. When my mother was not available, he expected me to do it. I guessed now his second wife had the honor. My father talked about magic tricks. I only half listened, thinking that it had been a mistake to invite him to my home.

"I rent a room, so I can practice my magic tricks and keep my props there. My wife is very orderly; I can't leave anything lying around in our apartment."

"That must be hard for you." I imagined how awful it would be to live with a woman who wasn't just orderly, but obsessive. He sighed.

"You are right. It is difficult. I have actually stopped taking my medication."

"You mean your blood-thinners?"

"Yes, I don't need them anymore."

"But you have had two heart attacks. You need to take this medication to keep your blood from clotting."

"Well, I don't need it anymore," he repeated. "Can I smoke a cigarette here?"

"Go right ahead." Unfortunately smoking was one of my father's bad habits I had inherited. One of the things that reminded me of him and that I did not like about myself. We both could not stop. I was not going to tell him how bad it was for him. I was not his mother. We both sat and smoked silently, watching the smoke curl up and rise to my wooden ceiling.

"Well, I have to go." He got up to leave. "I have to be home in time for supper or else she gets really angry." I nodded. "It was good we had this talk," he concluded.

"Take care of yourself." I walked him out, and we hugged goodbye awkwardly, but we hugged.

Two weeks later my phone rang loudly at four in the morning. I fumbled for the receiver, half asleep. Early morning calls are usually bad news. I was afraid it was about my grandfather, who had been in the hospital for weeks.

"Are you awake?" said my mother's voice.

"Yes. Is it grandpa?"

"No, but your father is dead."

"Dad?—but I just saw him. He seemed fine."

"It was very sudden. Another heart attack," she said.

I was awake now. My mind raced. I knew why my father had come to visit me.

That night, I found out the details of his death from my mother over a glass of whiskey. Whiskey felt like the right drink to commemorate my father.

He had gotten his wish: he died in a tuxedo.

My father and his wife were all dressed up for a fancy Magic Circle gala. It was two days before his sixty-third birthday. He dropped off his wife at the entrance of the ballroom so her dress shoes wouldn't get wet in the snow. He left to park the car. She waited and waited, but he did not appear. Finally she sat down for the magic performances. His seat remained empty. Acquaintances and friends asked about him. They went out to the parking lot to look for him, but he was nowhere to be found.

"He disappeared into thin air," one of his colleagues exclaimed with admiration.

His wife was hysterical. They finally found his car, but still no trace of him.

The evening went on without him, cocktails, dinner, and performances. A rumor spread through the crowd: "He vanished without trace. It's a magic trick."

"I didn't think he had it in him," his colleagues whispered, impressed.

Long past midnight, a friend drove my father's sobbing wife home. At three in the morning the police showed up at her door. They had traced his address through the medical card for blood thinners he carried. Except he did not take his medication anymore, and his blood was not thin. He had parked the car, suffered a fatal heart attack, and died. He was still in his formal wear—death had been quick and cold—a black tuxedo on white snow.

~

I didn't know any of the people attending his funeral. My mother and I sat in the back of the Lutheran church his second wife had chosen for the service. My father didn't go to church. He had been an agnostic. I looked at him in his tuxedo lying in the open coffin. *Don't look so smug,* I thought. *I know you got what you wanted.*

My mother squeezed my hand so hard I thought she was going to break my bones. It felt like the funeral of a stranger. My mother had been married to him for twenty years, and his second wife for only seven. Nevertheless, she was the star of this production. Two black-clad friends supported her on each side as she swooned down the middle aisle, sobbing and reaching out to the heavens. Maybe they had gotten married at this church. I did not know; I had not been invited. My father's second wife, dressed in an expensive black gown, managed to speak eloquently despite her grief. She praised him as the love of her life (all seven years of it) and as a brilliant, charming genius, a talented artist and entertainer. Watching her, it finally dawned on me why my father had made the effort to track me down, and why he had wanted to meet with me so urgently.

I didn't know this man she was talking about. I was surprised we were even invited. My mother must have felt the same way, because we left early. Nobody noticed.

~

"He wanted to die," I said to my mother as we crossed the deserted parking lot in front of the church.

"Nonsense, why would he have wanted to die?" my mother retorted angrily.

"Because he was unhappy. He could not bear living with that woman."

"You heard her, they were supremely happy."

"That's what she says. He told me he stopped taking his blood-thinners. He didn't want to live anymore."

"What rubbish," she replied. "He had everything he wanted. A young wife who adored him, his pension, time to travel ... I am the one who was left stranded."

As usual, I ignored her bitterness.

"I realize now that was the reason he came to see me. He told me he stopped the medication, and he was smoking again. He knew he wouldn't live much longer. He came to say goodbye."

"What are you saying? He smoked? What an idiot! I can't believe he smoked after two heart attacks."

"He chose to end it that way. I have to respect that he dies on his own terms. At least he did not suffer. Not like grandpa. Grandpa doesn't deserve such a long and painful death."

"You don't get the death you deserve; you get the death you can bear."

"In that case, I guess Dad couldn't bear very much. He had an easy death. He died in his tuxedo, as he always wanted."

13

MY DEAREST DEIRDRE ANN

APRIL BALDRICH

S he arranged the note on the pillow of her carefully made bed and headed to the foyer. Today Deirdre and her mother, Mishaela, would take a train downtown to Bergdorf's for shopping and lunch, one last time.

Deirdre walked the length of the dusty driveway, grateful for the gray, twisted shade and invigorating peppermint aroma provided by the California pepper trees. The sunbaked, isolated ranch was a far cry from her life in New York City, having more horses and almond trees than people and buildings. The open silence made Deirdre feel vulnerable, naked, as if all could see her soul and hear her thoughts. In her hand she clutched the letter.

As Deirdre came nearer the house, she caught sight of her aunt Felicia with her husband, Ramone.

"Deirdre Ann, my love, you have made it," Felicia squealed in delight.

Felicia's delicate features and well-coifed hair displayed that she was a blue-blood aristocrat in farmhand clothes. Deirdre's grandparents had been quite wealthy. They had left their fortune to their two daughters, Felicia and Mishaela. Mishaela had used her money to live a decadent life in the city, while Felicia used her inheritance to buy a Western ranch, far from decadence. Felicia had married the ranch hand Ramone twenty years prior, but they never had children of their own. Beyond Deirdre's summer visits to the ranch, Felicia didn't have patience for children.

"Ramone, fetch Deirdre's bags," Felicia chirped. Ramone snapped up straight in his boots, and tipped his old Stetson toward Deirdre.

"I didn't bring any bags." Deirdre's eyes focused on the dirt between Felicia's and Ramone's feet.

While Felicia showed Deirdre to her room, Ramone returned to the horses in the stable. His thoughts wandered to Deirdre as a child; the little ginger girl with pigtails roaming the almond groves, spinning stories of faeries and magic. Her free-spirited independence and tireless laughter were the mirror of Felicia's. To Ramone, Deirdre was the child he had always longed to have with his beloved wife. Mishaela's death had made that dream a reality.

"Ramone, aren't you getting too old to be tending the horses?" Deirdre popped through the stable door with a giggle.

"*Mija*, how are you holding up?" Ramone asked as he took the young woman in his arms and pulled her into a warm, protective hug.

"Thanks for visiting me in New York last month, Ramone. My own father never cared to help me with my alcoholic mother. I really needed your fatherly guidance to deal with her, and move on with my life. And now she's gone ..."

"Oh, my Deirdre, she was your mother, despite her faults. It's a difficult thing to live with."

"You know, it is what it is. She was many things, but never a mother ..." Deirdre trailed off. "However, Felicia has dinner ready, and sent me to fetch you!" The spark returned to Deirdre's voice.

⁓

Dinner was served on the patio on the old wooden long-table. Oil lamps illuminated the dusk. A cool breeze offered respite from the day's heat. The intimate family dinner, with its home preparation and notable lack of gin, was a pleasant change from the meals Deirdre was used to with her mother. As Ramone passed her the potatoes, Deirdre began to cry.

"Aw, my poor little Deirdre, you must be devastated." Felicia said, her voice cracking as the tears welled in her own eyes.

"It was horrifying," Deirdre started, as she had rehearsed a hundred times, "We had gone to Bergdorf's, as we did every Wednesday, but that day, instead of a town car, Mishaela wanted to take the train. Shopping went well; we had lunch, Mishaela had more than a few cocktails, as usual; and we headed to the train to return home. She wasn't steady. We waited for the train on the platform in silence. As the train rushed in, she started to lean forward. I tried to grab her, but there were so many people rushing past. She said 'You will not hold me back any longer.' With that, she leaped in front of the train. After all the police statements, I was brought home, where I found her letter on my pillow."

My Dearest Deirdre Ann,

Your father has moved on with his life, never to return to me. My responsibilities, as a mother, do not allow me to move on with my life. As I am not able to exist on my own terms, I will cease to exist at all.

Best Wishes,
Mom

Deirdre was no longer crying. Her eyes were wild with the telling of her tale.

"I guess old Mishaela should have 'minded the gap,'" Ramone chuckled while taking another drink of his merlot.

The color drained from Deirdre's face as Ramone clasped her clammy hand. Ramone could see his humor was in poor taste.

Felicia quickly changed the subject. "Well, Deirdre, it is getting late, and I was planning on us going into San Francisco tomorrow, take in the Fisherman's Wharf and such. Ramone and I will clean up; you go get some rest."

As they tidied up the patio, Felicia expressed her concerns, "*Mi amor*, I just don't know. Deirdre seems in denial; her words are steady, but her light is gone. Mishaela blamed her in the letter for her suicide. That is just unthinkable, even for a woman as cold as Mishaela."

"Mishaela was never one to take responsibility for her life, why should her death be any different? The world is a better place without her." Ramone said flippantly as he extinguished the oil lamps. "I shouldn't worry so much. I know Deirdre will be fine. Besides, you have the child you have always wanted, and Deirdre has the family she always wanted. Her light will return." Felicia sighed.

Ramone stared down at the last lit candle, entranced by its flicker. "Sometimes people just need a little push to get what they want in this world." And with that, he blew out the flame.

14

INTO THE FOG

CORNELIA FEYE

I stuck the garnet ring onto my mother's lifeless finger. Her coffin stood in a gray concrete cell cold enough to make me shiver. Or maybe it was the presence of death. My mother's skin stretched tightly over her cheekbones, and her face looked white as wax and small like a doll's. It lacked the wrinkles and lopsided contortions the spasms of the final stages of Parkinson's disease had sent through her body. She was no longer drooling and gasping for breath as her throat muscles shut down. Instead she looked more peaceful than I had seen her in years—young and innocent in the white nightgown with hands folded on her chest. The undertaker had combed her short hair caringly for her final appearance on earth.

I am glad you are finally at peace, I thought.

The few family members huddled together in the cold cell, wrapping their scarves around their necks. Soon the cold would be replaced with the searing heat of the crematorium oven. As a gesture of affection we laid flowers into the coffin to accompany my mother on her last journey.

~

I had found my mother's favorite garnet ring in the drawer of her nightstand. The ring was with her to the end. It had been a gift from my father, who had died twenty-five years ago, and even when he was still alive, they were not together. But she had kept the ring, and the memory of better times. I wanted her to take that ring with her. It had meant something to her, even after she had shed all other possessions.

Next to me I heard muffled sobs from my brother. Tears stung in my eyes too, but I did not allow them to flow. It was too easy. I did not want to cry and give in to self-pity. My mother was clearly better off now, so any tears I shed were only for myself. I wanted to be clear and aware during these last moments with my mother, or at least with her mortal body. I wanted to imprint her image into my memory as she was now to replace the tortured woman I had watched for years: the mother who still fought for every hard-earned breath and for every day of life in a body that had betrayed her terribly.

It was not the first betrayal of her life. There was the betrayal of her husband; the abandonment of her daughter, who left for America; her bosses, who never acknowledged her dedication to her work, but instead, fired her when she started shaking from Parkinson's disease. Her country had betrayed her in her youth, when it entered into a disastrous war following a madman. I hoped that she had worked through all these karmic knots and was now ready to let go.

"Ready?" asked Dani, the crematorium technician. He looked the part of a Goth death attendant with his pale face, black clothing, and spiked black hair. We nodded and said a final Hail Mary for her, a prayer she had always liked. I silently added a Buddhist mantra. I figured it couldn't hurt to cover all the bases.

We walked over to the cremation room and stood in front of the iron oven door. Dani wheeled in the coffin, now closed. He tapped me on the shoulder and asked to speak to me.

"The ring you put in her hand," he began. "We cannot incinerate it. It will melt into a little ball and then get stuck on the grid. I can keep it out and then lay it back into the urn after the ashes have cooled."

"Yes, please do that. Thank you."

He nodded curtly and set the coffin onto tracks that pulled them into the oven. When the doors opened, my brother sobbed loudly. Deeply imprinted images of fire and hell probably rose in his mind, and he did not want to give up the body of his mother to the flames. But there were no flames inside. The pine coffin disappeared into white-hot heat. No crackling fire, no hissing sound. My mother's remains pulverized noiselessly.

What a great way to go, I thought. Finally she was rid of that bothersome body so her soul could rise to the sky with the smoke, cleansed of any material burden.

We walked out of the concrete building into a gray November afternoon. Wet yellow and brown leaves clung to the ground. A few rays of sunlight escaped from the cloud-covered sky to illuminate the city stretched out before us. I felt a wave of memories wash over me as if a floodgate had been opened. For days I had tried to recall special moments with my mother but had been stuck with the image of her in her hospital bed gasping for air, choking, her body stiff with the cramps of Parkinson's. Now I could picture her again swimming in a forest lake, riding her bicycle across the fields in the summer, bending over me with concern when I was sick, sitting in her rocking chair stroking the black cat on her lap, looking out on the birch trees before the window. I squeezed my brother's arm.

"I'm so glad I can suddenly remember her as she used to be before her sickness," I said to my brother.

"Me too," he answered. "She had to die, to live again in our memories."

Six months later our family gathered on a boat to lower the urn with my mother's ashes into the ocean, as had been her wish. The fog hung low over the waves of the North Sea. We clutched our coats against the moisture in the air and the wind from the north. The boat pulled up close to the island where my mother had been happiest. We gathered starboard and watched the urn being lowered into the waves.

"It is made of salt and will disintegrate within a couple of days," the mate explained.

The ring, I thought. *The ring will fall out once the urn dissolves.*

"The ring," I whispered to my brother.

"I know. It will sink to the bottom of the sea."

"I like that," I smiled. We stared out at the waves silently.

"Maybe someone will find it," my brother mused.

"Maybe it will bring them luck," I wondered.

"More luck than Mom ever had."

The children, including my son Max, threw blue irises, my mother's favorite flower, into the water. I tried to watch them disappear beyond the waves, but the fog swallowed the urn and the flowers before they could sink. I had the vague feeling that my mother's presence had not vanished completely.

On a foggy day years later, my son Max and I sat in our car at the bottom of the hill that leads up to our house. The fog was so thick that I could not see my hand in front of my eyes. I tried to drive uphill, but the fog became so dense, it blinded me.

"This is no normal fog," I said to Max. "Something is wrong." I pulled over to the curb, afraid to drive any further, trying to figure out what to do.

"Max, can you walk up the hill from here?" I asked. "I think it is safer. I'll join you there with the car in few minutes, okay?"

He got out of the car and began walking. I watched until he was swallowed by the fog. Putting on the high beams did not improve my visibility; they only created a tiny bubble of light illuminating a few inches of road. At a snail's pace I crept along in eerie silence, as the fog had muffled all sounds. The sight of the streets and gardens of the neighborhood had also been swallowed by the gray soup.

Suddenly the fog lifted, as if a heavy blanket had been pulled away. Looking around, I found myself on a freeway moving toward an unknown destination. I didn't recognize my surroundings, and had no choice but to drive along with the stream of cars. Obviously I had gone too far, our house lay behind me, but I couldn't turn around; I had to try and make it to the next exit. A torrential rainfall dumped sheets of water onto the road, and even the bridges and overpasses didn't offer any cover and protection. In the distance, I saw burning buildings and great floods covered the ground. A terrible catastrophe must have had happened. All I could think was *Max, I have to get back to Max.* The car ploughed through deep puddles until it veered and lost traction. It swerved wildly and crashed into a sheer wall at the end of the road.

Dazed and in shock I scrambled out of the wreck, which had folded like an accordion. A deep cut on my leg bled, my clothes were torn and muddy, but I had to get back to Max.

The fields next to the freeway had turned into a swamp. Struggling through the wet grass I was soaked within minutes. *I have to get to Max.* Not far ahead I saw a small yellow bungalow surrounded by water, and figured I could make it that far, wading through the knee-deep mud. The structure seemed unaffected by the disaster, appearing like a small oasis amidst chaos. What was going on?

~

I knocked and entered a warm, dry room. A woman sat in a rocking chair, with a black cat on her lap. She smiled at me.

"Mom, what are you doing here?" I cried, after the shock of recognition.

"I have been waiting for you," my mother said. "There are towels in the bathroom.'

"Mom, I have to call Max." It was too much to take in, first

Armageddon outside, now my mother in the only intact structure around.

"First dry yourself and calm down," she said stroking her black cat, still smiling as if she had expected me.

"I can't calm down; I need to get to Max." I knew I sounded hysterical.

"You won't be any good to him like this," she said reasonably.

Looked down at myself I had to admit I was in bad shape; soaking wet, caked in mud, with a ripped skirt and only one shoe, a bleeding cut on my leg. I became even more desperate to reach Max. Hopefully he was safely at home. Hopefully the house was still standing.

The walls in my mother's bathroom were covered with yellow tiles, like the ones in our apartment when I grew up. I took a fluffy white towel out of the orderly cabinet and cleaned myself up, put a Band-Aid on the cut, and washed my face and legs. When I returned to the living room, my mother made tea in the built in kitchen. She turned around.

"That's better," she said. "Sit down.'

"I can't sit down mom. I have to call Max."

"You can't make calls from here," my mother insisted.

"Why not?"

"There is no outside line."

"What is going on outside? The floods, the fires. It is like Armageddon."

"Things are just dissolving," she explained calmly.

"Dissolving? The fog was so thick I could not even see my own hand in front of my eyes and the water came down in sheets from the bridges and overpasses. It's like the end of the world has come."

"It can be very frightening," my mother confirmed.

"Exactly, that's why I need to reach Max. I have to make sure he is okay. He will be terrified. I have to get back to him."

"You only just arrived," she said.

"I made a mistake; I should have walked up the hill with him."

"Aren't you glad to be here?" She had always been good at making me feel guilty.

"I am glad you are doing well and you seem to be comfortable and happy." In contrast I felt tense and anxious.

"Yes, I am quite content."

"But I have to get to Max; make sure he is alright. He is my son, Mom," I tried to explain.

"You are my daughter."

"But I am a grownup and Max is only a teenager. I need to make sure he is alright. If I can't call, I will just go back on foot." I knew this answer was inadequate, as my explanations for leaving had always been inadequate. Even if I needed to get to my son, I felt selfish. My needs were always more important than hers.

My mother looked at me with big eyes, surprised that I did not know what was so obvious to her.

"You don't understand. I am not holding you back, but you can't leave from here," she said in a determined tone, unusual for someone who had always been timid and insecure.

She handed me a mug with tea, and as I reached for it, I saw the garnet ring on her left hand reflecting the fading light.

15

INVIGORATED,

CLAIRE RANN

Momma sipped scotch every morning. Daddy drank it in bigger gulps—but later in the day, once he'd come home to me, Momma, and my four younger sisters.

But that's not why I did it.

It wasn't because Daddy was returning later each day, or because Momma had had *another* baby, on my eleventh birthday, no less. There was a six-year gap between me and Ruthie, the next in line, and after that there were three more.

The day of the "incident," as the adults would call it, little Edie was there too, just inches away. No one could blame her. Not even two yet, she could sit in the little blue plastic pool and pour sun-warmed water into teacups for hours.

That's why I'd gotten the kiddie pool out in the first place—not because I'd planned to do anything, like Momma would say afterward—but because it would keep little Edie out of my hair. Just the sight of the kids, with their silly games and constant whines, made me feel like I was wading through wet sand. I was bored to death as the unwilling helpmeet of unwanted company.

It was only nine that morning when Momma kicked us out of the house, the air already hazy with the summer heat. I was to mind

Ruthie and little Edie outside so as not to wake the baby and Katie, the other one, who was sick with a cough.

Little Edie sat and watched the whole thing, only glancing over when Ruthie's arms started splashing in and out of the water. Edie smiled at the droplets on her pale white skin. She still had that strange rubbery baby fat skin five-year-old Ruthie'd grown out of.

I'd noticed what they would call dark thoughts before, images that popped into my mind and sent pulses of energy through my fingers and toes. As I held a neighbor's gray kitten, I saw my thumb and fingers tightening around its neck and imagined feeling the snap of its toothpick bones. When Ruthie and I climbed the ancient elm in the neighbor's yard, I stared at her legs swinging as she sat below me, and pictured her body smacking against branches as she tumbled down.

"Bet you can't hold your breath for a minute," I said to Ruthie that day. A new picture had formed in my mind as the pool filled with hose water. No one was there to stop me.

"Can too," Ruthie said. Her eyes widened as she took in an exaggerated breath.

I pointed to the pool. "In there," I said, "so I know you're not cheating."

Ruthie stomped over to the pool and plunged her head in. I knelt at her side and pressed her head down, holding it hard against the plastic pool bottom. My heart raced.

I felt her forehead and nose flush against bumps of the uneven ground beneath the stiff plastic. I pushed harder, imagining the back of her skull giving in, flattening her head completely. In my mind's eye there hadn't been any blood, but the red swirls that appeared pleased me.

The water muffled Ruthie's screams, reducing them to bubbles disturbing the surface. Little Edie giggled at the water's agitation, reaching one chubby arm over to splash the bubbles floating along the top.

When Ruthie stopped twitching, I loosened my hold and felt her limp body rise in the water. Little Edie continued filling and spilling her teacup. Ruthie's stick-straight hair, darkened by the water, floated in a semicircle around her head. It wasn't precisely how I'd imagined, but I felt exactly how I'd thought: invigorated.

They want me to blame those ideas that pop into my head, want to make them disappear somehow. But I don't want them to leave. They are all I have these long, dull days, all the more so while I'm kept in this gray room.

They all keep asking me why, why I was so angry, what Ruthie or Momma or Daddy had done to make me want to hurt her. But it had nothing to do with them. I did it because it would feel good. I was bored, and then I wasn't. That's all.

16

MURDER 101

TAMARA MERRILL

A couple of years ago, at one of those big used book sales, I found a copy of short stories titled *100 Malicious Little Mysteries*. As I read it, I realized that the idea of getting away with murder fascinated me. To be honest I was more than fascinated. I was intrigued. Not every story in the book was about killing, but at least thirty or forty were brief, concise guides on ways to commit murder. One hundred percent of the stories that involved a homicide included either how the murderer got away with the murder or why the murderer was caught. And, obviously, if you know what went wrong it is simple to reverse engineer anything.

I started taking notes. I laid out a spreadsheet that included perpetrator, victim, sex of both, relationship to each other, motive, weapon, and mistakes made. Quickly I realized that I also needed to track how they got away with it and I added a column titled *Clever Actions*.

I skipped through the book, reading only the stories that were murder-related. Then I moved on to the Internet. Google gave me famous murders, unsolved murders, and a list of the top ten murder weapons and methods in the United States. Firearms were number one by far; then other weapons, including knives and something called weapons not otherwise stated. All very interesting, but what caught my attention were the statistics about unsolved murders. Thirty-five to forty-five percent of all murders in the United States go unsolved.

Researching the homicide statistics pointed out a few things that my reading of fiction had not. In the short stories, and in all those murder mysteries I'd read or watched on TV over the years, there was always a motive. In real life, as in books, the motive seemed to lead to the arrest of the murderer. So, I reasoned, it would be safest to murder with no motive, just choose a random victim and use a weapon that you can get rid of completely and quickly. But, I wasn't a weirdo, serial killer type; I just wanted to see if I could plan the perfect murder. I wouldn't actually kill anyone. However, if my plans were to feel real to me, my "victim" would have to be someone that I believed should be dead—I thought I'd need a motive.

I stalled at that point. There was the geeky kid in high school but he was now a multimillionaire and very high profile. I considered the bully from grade school. When I looked her up, I discovered that she'd been a suicide ten years ago or, I speculated, maybe she was one of those unsolved murders. My boss was a jerk. If I couldn't think of anyone else to use he might do, although he was so dumb it wouldn't be much of a challenge. My siblings were uninteresting. My parents had never abused me. I had a couple of exes that made it to my "maybe" list.

Saturday night I took a break from my new obsession and went out to the Quarter with friends. It was fun. We hit a few hot spots, drank a bunch of shots, and ended in a bar with a pool table, where Josie and I proceeded to wipe the floor with a couple of jerks. By the time the bartender announced "last call" my buddies had disappeared. I grabbed one last drink, waved goodbye to the pool jerks who were now my best friends, and headed home.

A thick fog had settled over the city. I bet I couldn't see five feet in any direction. I could hear voices and an occasional car, but everything was distorted. I moved next to the buildings and trailed my fingers along the wall, walking slowly so that I wouldn't bump into or trip over anything. I traversed Fifth and Sixth avenues, carefully and quickly, hoping that no one would run over me. It crossed my mind that, if I were driving in this soup, I could murder someone and claim it was an accident.

A glow in the fog told me I was at the river. I lived just across the bridge. I shivered. Thinking of murder had made me recognize that I was out here alone. I quickened my pace.

It was spooky on the bridge. The lights were closer together so the fog was brighter but no less dense. I really couldn't see my fingers in front of my face. "Hey," a voice spoke from right behind me. A hand landed on my shoulder.

I whirled and pushed against the chest of one of the poolroom jerks. He stumbled and hit the bridge rail. I didn't stop to think. I stooped and lifted his legs. He flipped backward over the concrete edge. There was a muffled cry and then a splash.

Fourth most popular murder weapon, I thought, personal weapons, including hands feet, head butts, pushing, etc. That wasn't hard at all, and it was perfect—no motive, no witness, and no weapon to get rid of.

I was a natural at murder.

17

GUARDIAN OF THE WATCHTOWER

APRIL BALDRICH

Magnolia sat cross-legged on the floor of her duskily lit bedroom. In her lap: a brand new copy of *Celtic Magik: An Encyclopedia of Rituals and Spells*. She took a deep breath and opened the cover.

"Only divine intervention can save my ass now." Her eyes cast a threatening slant. "Sweet Mother Goddess, do not let me down." She scanned through the table of contents: "Introduction: Aligning with the Power of the Natural World," "Gnomes," "Fairies," "Druid," "Daily Rituals," "Moon Phases" ...

"What the fuck, I don't have time for this shit, where is the goddamn 'Pass My Finals' spell?"

She distraughtly scrolled pages, "Love spells, money spells, luck spells, removing negativity, self-empowerment, gnome magik, fairie magik ... this is garbage. I'm a frickin' genius, and this is clearly written for weak-minded simpletons. I'll just pick out the elements I need from the tables in the back of the book, and make my own spell."

Magnolia set her genius skill of logical deduction to work. If rituals to increase positivity in your life worked best under the full moon, then they would work well enough under the new moon—

maybe even better. In lieu of the recommended "magical" herbs, she was fairly certain the salt, pepper, cinnamon, and Old Bay she had on hand would suffice. The goddess would understand that cypress stump and wolfsbane are not exactly items stocked at the local Kroger. The substitutions continued with academic precision: wand of birch—wooden spoon; purified candles of various colors—the ones in the drawer in case of a power outage; silver chalice—rinsed out Big Gulp cup. Seriously, the ancient Celts could not possibly have had access to all this fanciness; close enough.

With the necessary materials now acquired, Magnolia skimmed the twenty pages of standard purification procedures and opening rituals. She erratically tossed some salt on the floor and began to summon the Guardians of the Watchtowers, the spirits that guarded the four cardinal directions, or the natural elements of earth, wind, fire, and ... uhm ... water, and part of a Jimi Hendrix song.

"Hail to the Watchtower of the North. I hope it's cool that I started with you. I'm not trying to play favorites; so all the other guardians, I'll get to ya. Please watch over my ritual and help me pass my finals, especially physics; that shit's really hard."

Magnolia lit the white emergency candle, with the aluminum foil base, in honor of the Guardian of the North Watchtower, whoever the hell that is.

"Hail to the Watchtower of the ... okay, this is just weird and overly formal. East, West, South, just gather round. I'm tired and want to get a move on."

She lit the remaining three candles, which were positioned in reference to the four cardinal directions—more or less.

With the confidence of an ancient priestess, Magnolia conducted the ritual in her own idiom. She poured her "herbs" in the Big Gulp cup and stirred them with the wooden spoon that she had "cleansed" in the flame of one of the candles.

"Goddess of the awesomest power, please help me pass my finals this week, especially the one in just a few hours. Please do not fuck this up for me. Thank you for your kind attention on this matter."

She closed her eyes, inhaled the healing scent of Chesapeake fry cook, and meditated on passing her finals and becoming a model student in the quarter to come.

Hours later, Magnolia awoke to a foggy morning, no wiser in physics, to face the first of her finals. The good Goddess and Guardians of the Watchtowers failed to make a showing. She returned home in defeat, to the TV on full blast and her roommate's bedroom door shut. Figuring him to be napping, she turned off the TV, lay on the couch, and quickly fell into a deep sleep.

"S'up, Maggie!" Magnolia's roommate, Camden, yelled, as he burst through the front door.

"Jesus H. Christ!" Magnolia startled awake. "You haven't been home?"

Squinting his left eye, Camden tilted his head toward the only door to the apartment, which he had just entered. "I'm gonna go with a solid 'no.'"

"So you left the television on C-Span, volume full blast, for the benefit of an empty apartment today?" Magnolia stammered.

"Um. I'm gonna, also, go with a solid 'no' on this one."

"So, I am to understand that someone has broken into our apartment. Whilst we were at school. Neither stole—nor disturbed—anything. Watched the most boring television network on air—at deafening decibels. Then simply left—undetected—from a fifth floor apartment. With one way in and one way out. And didn't bother to flip off the tele?"

A bewildered Camden, frustrated by his own finals, snapped back at his Chihuahua of a roommate. "It was probably the same motherfucker that left a charred-ass spoon and a Big Gulp cup of nasty shit in our sink."

Magnolia rolled her eyes, "Whatever; you're a dick."

"Well you're a child." Camden defensively snapped.

Magnolia stormed into her room, slamming the door.

Through the closed door, she could hear his condescending voice, "Out of respect for others that have to live with your entitled ass, please refrain from setting the kitchen utensils on fire and leaving your rotting mess in the kitchen."

The following year would bring about changes and triumphs for Magnolia and Camden. Despite the rough finals week, she would go on to be a better student, and with the aid of summer school, she and Camden graduated. Their vests, adorned with plastic name tags, would be swapped for embroidered lab coats, and bills would be paid in a timely manner ... mostly. Between the new jobs and new activities, Camden and Magnolia, friends since grade school, saw less of each other. The first one to arrive home after work would turn off the blaring television, now a daily occurrence.

It was oddly bonding. A deaf ghost that's really into politics. He's annoying, but he's ours. Camden, not one to subscribe to ghosts, suspected Jorge, the maintenance man, was taking long afternoon breaks in the apartment, quickly dashing out when he heard someone on the stairs. It wasn't a strong theory, but fun, so they went with it. Whether, ghost, slacker maintenance man, or faulty wiring, the TV issue was dubbed the result of Jorge.

With the evolution of adulthood happening beyond their control, so did Jorge. Magnolia arrived home to find, not only the TV on, but the toilet and bathroom sink running. This, too, became common occurrence.

"Camden, Jorge is getting too damn comfortable here. Now he's coming and taking a shit." Magnolia couldn't say it without laughing.

Camden laughed his asthmatic laugh. "Maybe we should leave him some beer and snacks."

"Seriously though, Cam, I'm starting to feel creeped out in my room at night. It's like there's something looming over me. The TV has started coming on at 3 a.m. The pipes vibrate like a jackhammer in the wall. I don't know how all this doesn't wake you up?"

"Well, I'm a deep sleeper. You watch too many ghost shows. There's nothing in your room. I'll call the actual Jorge about the plumbing. I have a headache though, so I'm going to lie down."

That night Camden went out with friends, and Magnolia felt the full wrath of ghost Jorge. It started simply enough. The TV came on.

The water ran in the bathroom. Magnolia did damage control, turning off the TV and water, and went to ready for bed. There was a palpable heaviness in the air, a silence she could hear. Nothing grabbed her, but a force spun her full circle. Shaking, she grabbed her keys, and left. She drove, with no particular destination in mind, with the hope that Camden would be home later that night.

When she returned home, the TV was on and a light fixture was dangling by its wires from the wall. Exhausted from nights of vibrating pipes, she went to bed, leaving every light on. In her much needed slumber, she dreamt. She didn't know she was dreaming. An ominous presence consumed the room, blotting out the light. She couldn't leave her bed. Golf clubs from a hallway closet began flying into the room. Despite her paralyzing fear, she summoned the strength to crawl on the floor beneath the barrage of projectiles. She made it to Camden's room; he was in bed. She crawled in next to him, clung to him crying. "I'm not being weird, I'm just terrified right now."

She woke up, in her own room, to a knock on the door. Her room was in perfect order, no golf clubs or damage. She opened the door to find a timid Jorge, who stood a good half-foot shorter than her.

"You have problems with you bathroom, Miss Magnolia?"

"I do. The toilet and sink keep running, and the pipes are vibrating like a jackhammer," Magnolia said with a false air of command.

"I no hear nothing. You should move." Jorge's voice quivered slightly, as he signed the crucifix in the manner of a devout Catholic.

"Excuse me?" Magnolia questioned, taken aback by Jorge's statement and passive refusal to enter the apartment.

"Yeah, this neighborhood too expensive. I live south. Nice, big apartments, half the price."

"I like it here, and we work near here, so, um, we kinda wanna stay. But given the high rent, I do expect my plumbing to be taken care of for me."

"It not doing anything now ..." *Crank. Brrrrrr.* The walls shook with the grinding of the pipes. Jorge, still standing beyond the threshold (ironic, given they suspected he hung out in the apartment all day), made the sign of the cross again and said, "You need Jesus. I will send him." And with that, Jorge turned and all but ran down the stairs.

Shortly after, Camden came home, looking like a tomcat after a storm.

"Where have you been? You look like hell! Is that blood on your shirt?"

"My friend had VIP at Diamond Dugout. They kept giving me shots. I think I fell through a table. I woke up on someone's couch. I need to sleep."

"Jorge was here and wouldn't come in." Magnolia filled Camden in on the odd interaction. "He's sending Jesus, I guess?"

Camden, swaying, "Jesus, or Jesus, the maintenance manager?"

Magnolia laughed. "He wasn't really clear on that. I suppose we could use the help of both."

The next morning, Camden woke up, grabbed his golf clubs from the hall closet, and headed to the driving range. Jesus never arrived. Her phone rang that afternoon. The number was Camden's. She heard the crank of pipes on the other end of the line, and felt the force, the one that had spun her nights before, envelop her in a hug. The call disconnected and the TV flashed on.

Magnolia crossed the room and turned off the TV. Her phone rang again. This time the number was Camden's childhood home phone. The caller was his aunt. Camden was dead. It had been sudden, painless, and unexpected.

From that moment on, the TV remained dark and silent, his bathroom toilet and sink never felt the movement of water, and the pipes ceased their rattle forever. The ominous presence no longer loomed, and Magnolia was left alone in an impalpable silence she could not hear.

18

BLUE MOOD

CORNELIA FEYE

W hen she left the soot-covered city of Duisburg on Valentine's Day, Sarah was in a blue mood. She had exactly five euros in her pocket. Her only asset was an Interrail pass, which allowed her to take any train anywhere, anytime in Europe. Unfortunately it was expired. With ink and a little scraping, Sarah extended the expiration date for another three months. She had ninety days to travel anyplace she wanted. She could sleep on the trains, eat on the trains, think on the trains, dream on the trains, and let them carry her wherever they would lead—most importantly as far away as possible from Harry.

Inside the drafty station building Sarah took one look at the timetable and picked the next train going south. Twenty minutes later, it left form platform 11. She deposited her shoulder bag on the overhead shelf and sank into a faux leather seat in a compartment for six.

When the train began to move, her shoulders relaxed, and the tension drained out of her body. As the speed accelerated, Sarah felt her energy and thoughts flow in unison with the movement. The rhythm of the wheels turning on the tracks set the gears of her mind in motion. The bleak landscape of the German industrial region flitted by just fast enough to turn into a pleasant blur. It felt good to be on the move; it felt good to get out of that awful city; it felt good to be alone.

Each turn of the wheels carried her a little farther from the miserable self she had been. She had been delusional, thinking Harry was her Prince Charming. *How much time of our lives do we spend inside an illusion? Most of it?* Sarah looked at the wet industrial buildings rolling by outside, blackened from smokestacks, spouting dark soot into a leaden sky. This was reality, without illusion. If she had to face reality, at least she could do it in a warmer and more pleasant climate. The train headed to Zürich, where she could change to another one going across the Alps, maybe to Italy. Yes, Italy would be nice. She could always think so much clearer while moving.

After arriving at this conclusion, Sarah looked around her compartment and realized that another passenger had entered while she drifted in her daydream. A blond girl, Sarah's age, occupied the window seat across from her. She had pulled her hair back from her chubby, pretty face into a tight ponytail, and stared outside while eating a sandwich. An apple and a soda sat on the small tray-table underneath the window. Sarah realized she was famished. She could not even remember the last time she had eaten. Probably before Harry kicked her out of the apartment after noticing some of his dope was missing. Her stomach grumbled. The blond girl looked up and smiled at Sarah. *She must have heard my stomach*, Sarah thought.

"Would you like half of my sandwich?" the girl asked in a Nordic accent.

Sarah nodded.

"Thank you. I am Sarah."

"Krista." The girl handed her a neat triangle of white bread with ham and cheese, which Sarah wolfed down in a few seconds.

"It's very good," she said apologetically.

"No, it isn't," replied Krista. "You are just very hungry."

"It tasted good to me."

Krista smiled. "Where are you going?"

"South, I don't know exactly. Maybe Italy. What about you?" Sarah said vaguely.

"Rome," Krista said in a quiet voice, as if talking about a romantic secret.

"Rome sounds good." Sarah imagined the eternal city in her mind: shady gardens and great art; Italian espressos and dolce vita.

"What are you doing in Rome?"

"I am going to attend a circus workshop."

"A circus workshop?" Sarah perked up. She could not picture Krista in her creased jeans and conservative linen blouse as a circus performer.

"It is actually more a theater workshop, with classes in dance, pantomime, and improvisation. A famous Swiss circus clown is the director," Krista explained.

"No kidding." Sarah regarded Krista with new respect.

"I took it last year and loved it so much that I worked all year in a really boring job at a Laundromat so I could attend again this spring."

"Where are you from?" Krista now had Sarah's full attention.

"I am from Upsalla, in Sweden. Where are you from?"

"I don't know any more where I am from. I am from many places. I came back from India recently." Sarah omitted her stay in the soot-covered town of Duisburg.

They both sat quietly for a few moments. Sarah pictured Roman circus clowns, while Krista probably tried to imagine Indian beaches.

"Do you want to come to Rome with me?" Krista finally asked. "You could stay with me for a while, until you find something else. I am renting a small place in Trastevere."

Ancient ruins, ornate churches, fountains, piazzas packed with cafés and colorful people flashed through Sarah's mind. Where else was she going to go? She had no plan, nobody was waiting for her.

"Sure," Sarah said, after the smallest of hesitations. "That sounds great."

A narrow bed, wooden chair, and a small table were crammed into Krista's room at the pension in Trastevere. It looked more like a closet than a bedroom—a charming closet. Sarah slept on a mattress on the floor. She didn't mind. Their window looked out onto a narrow lane off the Piazza di Santa Maria de Trastevere, where men in light suits and women in sundresses sat in street cafés and bars in the mild February sun. Sarah fell in love with Rome.

She met the circus clown, Rolf, the next morning when she walked Krista to her class at the studio on the Gianicolo, one of Rome's seven hills. A ring of frizzy red hair surrounded Rolf's balding head. A short, portly man, with a big smile and huge hands, he looked like a circus clown even without makeup. His striking assistant, Mara, at least a head taller and a decade younger, smiled condescendingly at Sarah. Sarah beamed back her most radiant smile. Rolf looked at both of them and burst out laughing. Despite his physical shortcomings, he had a charismatic personality, spoke French, German, Italian, and English fluently, possessed unlimited energy and imagination, and saw the humor in his observations of human weakness.

Krista introduced her friend: "This is Sarah. She just came back from India. She wanted to meet you and see the studio. Unfortunately she cannot participate in the workshop right now."

Rolf's eyes sparkled. "You are broke," he beamed at Sarah.

"An accurate assessment," Sarah confirmed.

"I might have a little job for you. Come back here at two."

He turned and bounced into the studio. Rolf's assistant Mara did not smile anymore. Her eyes shot daggers at Sarah.

At two o'clock, Rolf, the clown and workshop director, offered Sarah a job cleaning his and Mara's apartment.

"Sure," she said.

Being a cleaning woman had not been Sarah's ambition, but it amazed her how much she could learn about the inhabitants from the details of their domestic arrangement. Rolf and Mara slept in separate bedrooms, despite their public appearance as a couple.

Sarah picked up Mara's clothes and makeup tissues every morning in her messy room. Rolf usually made his narrow bed before she came, and he left his books and clothes neatly folded and stacked. The book titles on his bedside table ranged from Hermann Hesse to Friedrich Nietzsche, which Sarah applauded. When she arrived for work on her third day, Rolf and Mara waited for her in the hallway. They looked serious.

"Is this the inquisition or have I neglected to dust the top of the wardrobe?" Sarah asked. They didn't crack a smile.

"I wish dust was the only problem," Mara said sternly. Sarah's eyes widened. "My amethyst ring is missing."

"You think I stole it?" Sarah's heart started to race. "You have been kind to me; you offered me a job, a chance. You think I would repay you by stealing from your nightstand?"

"Ah, how did you know it was on my nightstand?" Mara snapped.

"I didn't. I never saw your ring."

"Sorry, Sarah," Rolf interjected, "but don't come back."

She hung her head. "I didn't steal from you." She had resisted the temptation to slip a banknote on the counter into her pocket. She barely made enough to eat, and Krista complained about the cramped conditions in their room every day.

"I knew she couldn't be trusted." Mara walked away briskly.

"She hates me," Sarah told Rolf.

"Love and hate are only two faces of the same coin," he admitted cheerfully.

At two o'clock, Sarah huddled on the stone bench in front of the studio like a wilting flower. The motley crew of students streamed out. About half were Italian, with the addition of a French mime, a German filmmaker from Berlin, four Americans, and one Swede—Krista. She sat down next to Sarah.

"What happened?" The German filmmaker, Maggie, a generous, expansive woman, sat down on her other side.

"I am going to jail. Mara wants to call the cops on me." Sarah told them the whole story.

Immediately Maggie offered to hide Sarah in her spacious suite at a small hotel on the Campo de' Fiore.

"You just met me, why would you invite me to move in with you?" Sarah asked perplexed.

"I like your spirit," Maggie said. "And I have too much space just for myself. I also don't like Mara."

"But how can you trust me? I was just accused of stealing a ring."

"You said you didn't do it."

"You believe me?"

"Yes, shouldn't I?"

Sarah thought for a moment. Was she trustworthy? Did she trust herself?

"I would like to do something for you, if you are so kind as to take me in," she said instead.

"What can you do?"

"I can read tarot cards."

"You read the cards?" Maggie asked excitedly. "That's perfect."

Sarah gave her a reading immediately after they arrived at the hotel room. Maggie drew the *High Priestess*. This card delighted Maggie, since she aspired to stay in tune with her feminine soul and intuition.

Sarah soon had a small business reading tarot cards. The students took her out to lunch or dinner for readings. She ate well and got to know them intimately. Even Rolf met her in the back room of a restaurant, far from Mara's suspicious eyes. Not surprisingly, *The Magician* emerged as Rolf's dominant card. After all, in one of his most successful tricks he sawed Mara in half on stage.

At a small café on the Piazza Navona under a Renaissance blue sky, Sarah held a reading for Pierre, the French mime. A slight, agile man, Pierre had a sparkle in his eyes, blue as cornflowers in the fields, and a mop of hair, blond as wheat. Sarah put Pierre's considerable miming skills to the test, since Pierre's English was as limited as Sarah's French. He drew the card of the *Page of Cups*. In broken French and English, Sarah explained that the card represents manifested imagination. A fish symbolizes a work of art emerging from the water of emotions to show itself to its creator.

Enthusiastically, Pierre turned around in a delighted pirouette and took a deep bow in front of Sarah. With a flourish he held the cards out to her.

"No, I cannot do them for myself. It does not work and it would be bad luck," she declined sadly.

With insistent gestures he presented a fan of cards to her again.

Sarah laughed and chose a card, which turned out to be the *Ace of Cups*.

Wordlessly Pierre pointed out how their cards were related. He compared the single chalice in both cards, and the blue water, streaming from Sarah's cup into a lily pond below. A white dove hovers on top of the overflowing goblet.

"It is a gift," Sarah explained. "A gift from the sky."

Pierre nodded and jumped onto his chair in one smooth movement to the great astonishment of the other café guests. He unrolled a scroll with old-fashioned handwriting. "A gift must be passed on," it announced.

"Pass it on?" Sarah asked.

Pierre beamed and mimed how the gift would die, if they did not share it. This made sense to Sarah, but she still was not sure what he meant.

"How can we pass it on?" she asked.

Pierre demonstrated a performance of the blue fish, the blue man, and the cup that overflows.

"The final performance," it dawned on Sarah. At the conclusion of the workshop, groups of students presented a short performance on the Piazza Navona. Pierre jumped up and down on his chair triumphantly.

Several guests at the café briefly turned their heads in their direction, but then returned to their espresso and conversations. This was Rome after all. People did strange things.

"But I am not even part of the class," Sarah considered.

Pierre made a sad face.

"And I have to hide from Mara, or I will land in jail."

Pierre held the blue napkin in front of his face.

"A mask? But why blue?" she asked.

Lifting the napkin, Pierre smiled, pointed at the sky, pointed at the water in the fountain, pointed at his eyes.

"A blue performance. I like it. No words, just gestures." Sarah leaned back in her chair and scanned the Piazza Navona, where the performance would take place. Three uniformed carabinieri turned the corner behind Neptune's fountain and came straight toward her.

"Pierre, I have to go, it's time for my daily prayers." She got up and dove into the Church of Nostra Signora del Sacro Cuore, whose simple white façade faced the piazza. The dark interior felt like a momentary sanctuary from the policemen outside.

Excitement built at the studio as the students got ready for their final performances. Costumes were secretly assembled, props procured and hidden. Each imaginative pantomime had to be a surprise and transcend the various languages. Some students played instruments. Maggie, Krista, and an Italian girl planned to perform one of Sarah's tarot cards, the *Three of Cups*, depicting the dance of the three graces with multicolored veils. Props, masks, secrecy, and costumes helped Sarah to stay undercover, but it was not easy to avoid Mara. Once she barely escaped her grasp by diving into a pile of costumes and pretending to be a mannequin wearing a golden mask.

On April First, the day of the performance, the Piazza Navona glistened in the spring sunshine. Unsuspecting tourists and pedestrians paused in amazement as jugglers, jesters, and magicians in colorful costumes set up what looked like a medieval fair. Finally the trumpets sounded, and Rolf, as Master of Ceremony, in a magnificent red velvet robe, announced the beginning of the show. The crowd of spectators grew, as dancers, mimes, and tricksters took the stage, amazing and delighting the audience. Sarah was so nervous, she could hardly breathe. She was terrified the tricks wouldn't work, that she would drop the props, or stumble on the cobblestones. As the last act, Pierre and Sarah emerged from the fountain, in wet robes clinging to their thighs, their faces painted blue like Indian gods, carrying a basket and a covered golden goblet on their heads. Mara gasped when she saw Sarah rising from the water. Sarah paled underneath her face paint. *I dare you call the cops on me now,* Sarah thought. *I disappeared from your view, only to resurface from the fountain as a blue magical being.* Pierre and Sarah handed out a round of flowers from the Campo de Fiori as offerings and threw sparkling blue beads into the crowd.

As the spectators accepted their gifts, a hushed silence took hold of them. The atmosphere changed from a noisy medieval fair to meditative calmness. Time seemed to stretch and expand as Pierre emptied his cup of water. Despite draining it to the last drop, a white dove emerged and ascended into the cloudless sky. The crowd sighed. Only the water dabbling in the fountain flowed through the silence like a single note from a flute. For a moment time stood still. The plaza seemed more spacious and the sky a deeper shade of blue. Sarah balanced on one leg, the golden cup on her head. Her mind went blank. She stood suspended, without a thought in her mind, just present there and then. The cup bubbled over and a fish jumped over its rim into the fountain with a little splash. The spell broke and the crowd applauded. Sarah woke as if from a trance, and took her bows with Pierre, while euro notes rained onto the cobblestones.

"It is a success!" Rolf declared and invited all the students in their costumes to dinner at the corner *ristorante*. The Italian students cried and lay in each other's arms with tears of joy about the successful performance and tears of sadness about their impending departure.

The German, English, and Swedish students expressed their emotions with more restraint. Pierre kept hugging Sarah, trying to convince her that she had a promising career as a street performer in her future. He shared the bounty from the performance, stuffing banknotes into her pocket. His blue eyes sparkled, and his blond hair flopped as he jumped, turned, and flitted from one person to the next like quicksilver. Sarah felt delighted about the performance and sad it was over. The students had become a substitute family. The next morning they would all disperse in different directions. After impersonating a magical being, what could go wrong now?

A lot, she realized, as she noticed Mara watching her like a hawk. It was high time to catch another train. This time she was running from a circus princess and the Roman police, but at least she had fifty euros and an amethyst ring in her pocket.

19

ONLINE DATING

TAMARA MERRILL

I t is Saturday night and Sharon has decided to try online dating. Everyone seems to be doing it. Wherever she goes someone knows someone who has met someone perfect that way. Of course, the women in her book club who have tried it admit that there are more jerks than standup guys but they keep trying. Last week Sharon's mother told her to "get her rear in gear" and give it a go.

At thirty-eight, Sharon thought her family had resigned themselves to her spinsterhood. Her grandmother had stopped asking if she was a lesbian, her brother had no more unmarried friends he was trying to fix up, and when her father called, he never asked about anything but the weather. Now her mother was back in mother mode sending her sample profiles and web site suggestions.

To be perfectly honest, Sharon admits to herself, *I'm bored and I need to get out more.* She pours a double shot of scotch over ice, sits on the sofa, clicks on the TV to *Forensic Files* and says "dating sites overview" into the microphone on her laptop. Immediately the screen springs to life. Sharon scans down the first page of results. A listing for Types of Dating Sites seems like a good place to start. Eleven categories are listed: Adult/Sexual Relationships, Christian Singles, Interracial Relationships, Korean Singles, Mobile Dating, African

American Singles, General Dating, Jewish Singles, Latin American Singles, Russian Singles, Wealthy-Affluent Individuals.

"Well," Sharon says out loud. "Not sure that this helps." She taps her search bar again and asks for, "Best singles dating sites." A listing for the Top 5 appears, which seems much more manageable, and she clicks on it;

1. Zoosk—Best for Matchmaking
2. Match—Meet the Most
3. OurTime—Mature Persons
4. eHarmony—For Marriage Minded
5. EliteSingles—Focus on Compatibility

Sharon ponders a minute, thinking about taking a flyer on one of these links. She has never heard of Zoosk; OurTime is out—she's not that mature; eHarmony is too Christian based; Match is a maybe and so is EliteSingles. She decides to search for another opinion and finds a chart showing the most successful dating sites. Xpress is at the top of the list.

If I'm doing this I might as well put myself on a successful site, she thinks, and types Xpress into the search. She enters her email and after four tries finds a username that isn't already in use. She submits, does the verification demanded, and the screen lights up with a very good-looking young man, shirtless and grinning enticingly. *"Want to fuck me?"* appears across his naked chest. "Yikes," Sharon gulps from her glass and hits the X to close the screen. She's not ready for that kind of dating site.

As she watches the middle aged detective on *Forensic Files* explore the reason for not arresting the guy she knows committed the crime, Sharon's thoughts wander back to online dating. She knows that some sites are all about hooking up. But surely they can't all be.

She decides to take another look at what's available. Plenty of Fish sounds good. It advertises as being free and lets her in to search without having to input any information. The first face up is someone she's seen around the office. *Holy shit, that would be awkward.* She tries PerfectMatch. Based in Seattle and modeled on the Myers-Briggs test. Now this might have possibilities; Sharon clicks on the link. The screen reveals that PerfectMatch is gone for good, but it suggests Friend Finder. That's enough. Sharon turns off her computer and switches the TV to Netflix.

On Sunday morning, Sharon finds her inbox full of emails from dating sites. "Damn Google," she says to her cat. Sharon pours herself a cup of coffee, and stands at the counter as she scrolls through the list, deleting all that include phrases with *F**** and *Hot* in the subject line, which leaves her with an ad for OKCupid, an email from her mother, and an ad from Macy's. She closes the laptop and goes to take a shower.

After a quick trip to the market and a long stop at her favorite coffee place (where no one said hi or even made eye contact), Sharon is back at her laptop. "I'm doing this," she tells her cat. The cat, whose name is actually Cat, jumps down from the windowsill and leaves the room.

Sharon opens OKCupid and quickly fills in the required info. Even before she finishes the profile questions, messages begin arriving. Looks like I'm not the only one that's bored on Sunday afternoon, she reasons.

The first message is from HuggyBear, "Hey, good looking. Want to meet for a drink and get to know me." Sharon notes that he's sixty-eight and in Memphis. Definitely GU (geographically undesirable). She types a quick response: "No thanks. You're too old and GU."

Message two is from NiceGuy168. Obviously this guy couldn't think of a clever user name but he is from San Diego and is reporting himself to be forty-six. The tiny picture looks okay but the message is full of misspelled words and mangled phrases. Sharon responds anyway with a brief "Thanks for your message."

1880white tells her how beautiful she is and what a lovely smile she has and asks for her phone number. Sharon skips to PlatoKnows who actually spells everything correctly, tells her he is a professor at a small college, and asks questions that expand on her profile. She is kind of impressed and composes a full answer to each of his questions.

Skimming through the next eight messages, she sends simple thank-you notes to five of them and deletes the other three. Answers start popping up and Sharon opens each one. Most are compliments on her smile and requests for her phone number.

Cat reappears and listens as Sharon says, "I don't get it. I thought you talked online for a while and then met in person." Cat kneads her leg and Sharon scratches behind Cat's ears. "Why would I give out my phone number or email address to people I don't know?" Cat yawns impressively and leaps off the sofa and heads to the kitchen in search of food. Sharon stands up and follows her.

All afternoon, as Sharon does her laundry, tidies her apartment, and gets ready for the week, a part of her brain is thinking about the messages. It was kind of exciting to get so many. It's been a long time since she flirted with anyone.

She makes herself a sandwich and turns on *60 Minutes*. Her laptop seems to be yelling at her, and she flips it open. The OKCupid site is still up. She is astonished to find twenty-six new messages and thirty-three likes. Sharon feels like the most popular girl at the party.

She has no idea what she should say in response. She decides to go with clicking first on each guy's picture, which will enable her to read his profile. It proves to be a good idea. Most of the profiles are incomplete but several focus on the desire for a "full, close relationship." Sharon assumes that this means sex first and get to know you later, and decides not to answer anyone who mentions politics, religion, or the need for a close relationship. Following the guidelines on the site, she composes a message carefully, one she can use for everyone: Hi—thanks for noticing my picture. I'm new to online dating but would love to hear more about your experiences on this site. I noticed in your profile that you ...

"There," she says to Cat, "that ought to do it." Clicking back and forth between the messages and the profiles she pastes her response into each, changing the profile remark each time. Almost at once Cowboy94 pops up in the Online Now window.

Cowboy94: Hey Sharon. How are you this evening?

Sharon: Hi. All good here; just watching TV and reading messages?

Cowboy94: Me too. I'm in El Cajon. Where do you live?

Sharon: Down by the beach.

Cowboy94: Which beach?

Sharon: Mission.

Cowboy94: Lucky you. Give me your phone number and I'll call you.

Sharon: I'd rather talk online first.

Cowboy94: I don't want a pen pal.

The chat window flickers and Cowboy94 is gone. She clicks her way through the rest of the messages. Two are from men in the armed forces, one is too young, and the other just right. She takes the time to write a nice response; it seems like a friendly, polite, thing to do. The message icon blinks, and she clicks back. There is a new message from PlatoKnows. Sharon opens the message. He's charming and articulate, answers her questions, and asks a few open-ended questions of his own, including asking the title of the book she is currently reading. He tells her that he enjoyed *All The Light We Cannot See* and asks her opinion. Sharon grins at Cat. "This is more like it," she says. Cat bats at her arm, requesting a head scratch. Sharon obliges and then composes her reply. She hits the send button and watches hopefully, but the chat window doesn't light up and it's time for bed anyway.

On Monday, Sharon goes to lunch with her friends. The others discuss their husbands and lovers but she doesn't mention online dating. She's a little embarrassed and not sure she wants anyone to know. Back at her desk, she sneaks a peek at the OKCupid site. There is a new message from PlatoKnows, but her boss is hovering and she's afraid to open it. It takes forever, but finally the day ends and she hurries home, feeds Cat, and logs on. Again his message is charming, witty, and smart. She begins to type, trying to be as clever as possible. The chat window lights up and he's online.

PlatoKnows: Are you there?

Sharon: Hi. Yes. I'm here. Just got home from work.

PlatoKnows: What type of work to you do?

Sharon: I do fund-raising research for a clinical research labora-tory? What do you do?

PlatoKnows: Interesting. You must be smart. I'm a teacher. Philos-ophy, at a college.

Sharon: I should have guessed from your name. LOL

PlatoKnows: It's probably kind of pretentious, but my real name is Harry and I couldn't think of anything clever using that since Harry Potter was already taken.

Sharon: Harry is a nice name. Very respectable.

PlatoKnows: Well, it's actually Harold, but my dad uses that so I've always been called Harry.

Sharon: Lovely, I wasn't named for anyone. My mom just liked the name. I see you live in Idaho. That's a long way from where I live.

PlatoKnows: Distance and age don't really matter, or even looks, although your pictures are lovely. I'm much more interested in meeting someone who makes me laugh and enjoys my company.

Sharon: Thank you. I found your pictures and profile interesting, too. I've only been on this site for a couple of days. Have you been online dating long?

PlatoKnows: About 6 months. I've been out with a few women but haven't really clicked with anyone yet? Would you like to switch to email? It is easier to write in full sentences and then when you are comfortable we can talk on the phone. My email is PlatoKnows@yahoo.com.

Sharon: Good idea. I'll send you an email in a bit. My email is sharon2543@gmail.com.

PlatoKnows: Perfect. I'll watch for it. Have a nice evening.

Sharon: Thank you. You, too.

Plato disappears from the chat window. Sharon sighs and runs her fingers through her hair. *That was fun, sort of.*

Sharon calls her friend Jeff. "So," she says when he picks up the phone, "tell me about online dating."

"Hello to you, too." Jeff laughs, a deep rumbling sound. "Is this an emergency, or are you trying to decide if you are finally going to try it?"

Sharon admits that she has been trying it over the weekend and confesses that she found someone of interest. "But how do you know?" she demands.

"It's just like meeting someone anywhere else. You have to take a leap of faith. I mean don't give out too much information right away, but you have to share something."

"I gave him my email."

Jeff chuckles. "Not a problem. I was thinking more of your home address. Did he ask for your phone number?"

"No. A bunch of other guys did, but I didn't give it to anyone."

"You're going to need to talk to him, you know. Find out if you have anything in common. I think you should send him a message and include your phone. If he's interested, he'll call you."

They talk a bit longer and Sharon hangs up, reassured that meeting someone this way is normal and acceptable. She writes an email to Harry, telling him a few things about her life and asking questions about his, adds her phone number, pushes send, and calls it a night.

At 7 p.m. the next evening, Sharon receives a very respectful text message:

Hi. This is Harry. Is this a good time to call?

She pushes Cat onto the floor. Runs a hand through her hair, checks her lipstick, and types back

Perfect.

It's as if they were old friends. The conversation roams from what they do for work, to books they've read, to hiking and favorite foods. Sharon has never felt so comfortable with anyone she's met at a party or a bar, and when she tells Harry he agrees. They talk for over an hour and agree to talk again tomorrow.

When they hang up Sharon Googles the college where Harry teaches. She's sure he's exactly who he says he is, but she is relieved to see that the picture in his OK Cupid profile is the same as his faculty picture.

Over the next week they talk every day and occasionally send a quick text. Neither of them has been married or has children. Sharon learns that Harry is trying to live "green" and she tells him that she'd like to do the same, but living in a big city makes it hard. He encourages her and gives her practical suggestions. On Saturday, Harry talks about spending the whole day berry picking and how on Sunday he will turn the berries into jam. He mentions that he also plans to can some tuna.

Sharon laughs incredulously. "Can tuna!" she exclaims. "How do you do that? Do you catch it yourself?" Harry sounds a little defensive when he tells her that he buys the tuna fresh and processes it in to half-pint jars. Sharon quickly stops laughing and apologizes for her reaction. "I'm sorry, Harry. It sounds amazing. I just had this image of you sticking tuna into those little cans. I have no idea how to make jam or can tuna. About the only cooking I do is to make a piece of avocado toast in the morning."

The conversation returns to an easy rhythm, and Harry asks, "Where do you want this to go? I usually date women who live close to me. But I'm willing to come to you if you'd like to meet in person."

"I would like to spend time with you," Sharon admits. She wonders how the sleeping arrangements would work out but has no idea how to ask what he has in mind.

"Lovely," Harry says. "I'll look at logistics and we can talk about details next time." Sharon agrees and they say goodnight.

She calls Jeff and blurts out her excitement. "Easy, girl." He laughs at her but tells her to enjoy the moment.

Sunday Harry doesn't call. Sharon waits until 8 p.m. and then sends a text:

How'd the jam turn out?

His text comes back an hour later.

Was just thinking of you. It took all day but I have 6 pints of blueberry and 4 pints of blackberry and 9 jars of tuna.

She responds

Wow! :-)

There is no answer.

All day on Monday, Sharon obsesses; she tells herself to stop but she doesn't. She hates being so unsure. By the time she reaches her apartment she's convinced herself Harry will never call again. "You'd think I was sixteen," she tells Cat. She makes herself a plate of apples and cheese and pours a large glass of wine.

The phone rings and she jumps but saves the wine from spilling. It's Harry. He seems perfectly normal, what in the world was she worrying about?

"By the time I cleaned up my mess in the kitchen last night it was way too late to call you."

"Not a problem, I was reading a good book and the evening flew by," she lies.

"I spent some time looking at flights and dates to come down to San Diego. But I have a little problem."

"Oh," Sharon tries to sound encouraging—not judgmental.

"I don't think we've talked about it, but I actually live with my older sister. She's disabled, and if I come down I need to find someone to care for her. She's been having kind of a rough time the last few days, and I hate to leave her with just anyone. Her friend that usually helps is in Europe for a couple of months."

"Have you been caring for her long?" Sharon asks. She wants to know what kind of disability the sister has and what kind of care she requires, but it feels like it would be impolite to ask.

"About fifteen years. Our parents died when I was seven and she was nineteen. She took care of me until I graduated from high school." Sharon murmurs sympathetically, and Harry continues, "Fifteen years ago, there was an accident that killed her husband and left Josie disabled so now I take care of her."

Sharon chooses her words carefully. "That's great. Family is so important. I'm not sure my brother would take care of me if something happened."

"I'm sure he would." Harry pauses and changes the subject. "Anyway, I don't think I can come down until our friend is back in town, so it will be about three months. I'm sorry."

"There's nothing to be sorry about. Maybe I can come up to see you?"

"If you did"—Harry sounds excited—"we have an extra bedroom. You'd have to share the bathroom with me, but I'm pretty tidy."

Sharon laughs. "Not a problem. I grew up sharing with my brother, and he wasn't tidy at all. I wouldn't want to disturb your sister. I could get a hotel for a couple of days."

"She'd love to have company. Since it's gotten so hard for her to get out, I try to bring the world to her. Someone new would be fun."

"Are you sure?"

"Absolutely. And, don't worry about me either. There won't be any pressure to take this relationship anywhere you don't want it to go." He pauses. "We'll just take it slow and get to know each other." Sharon smiles. It feels like he read her mind. Harry adds, "I'd be happy to pay for your plane ticket."

"Thank you for offering, but I travel for my job so I have lots of miles. I'll use some of them for a mini-vacation with you. Let's choose a date."

They compare calendars and talk about how long the visit should be. They agree that two days are not enough but that a full week might be too long for a first date. They laugh and settle on a Thursday through Monday visit. Harry doesn't teach on Friday, and Sharon will only need to take two days off work. Since neither one has anything pressing, they agree that if Sharon can get a flight she'll come right away, in only two days. After they hang up, Sharon dances Cat around the room. She can't remember when she's been this excited. She considers calling her mom but decides to wait until she gets home from her date. She calls Jeff instead, who says, "You go girl!" and offers to feed Cat.

The two days fly past as Sharon scrambles to decide what to wear and what to bring with her. She tries to think of an appropriate gift for Josie and settles on scented soap. *Not very imaginative, but everyone likes pretty stuff.*

On Thursday, Sharon tells Cat goodbye and catches a Delta flight to Boise. She's never been to Idaho before, and she's certainly never gone on a date like this. There isn't much to see out the window, but she can't concentrate on her book. The plane touches down, and her stomach flips. *Maybe this wasn't such a good idea.* Pulling her bag, Sharon walks quickly, looking around. She doesn't see anyone who looks like Harry. A man holds up a sign and waves to her. She realizes the sign has her name on it. She smiles tentatively, and the man grins.

"You look just like your picture," Harry says and pulls her into a hug. Sharon steps back, she isn't sure what to say. Harry helps her, "I know I don't look much like my picture. I don't photograph well, but it's really me."

Sharon laughs. "Well, you do look a little different, but you sound just like you do on the phone." She studies him for a moment. He looks a little older and heavier and there is something different about his hair, or maybe his eyes, she isn't quite sure.

"Come on"—Harry takes her hand—"let's get acquainted. It's about an hour's drive to Ontario, and then the house is about fifteen miles further, on a dirt road."

"You really do live out in the country," Sharon laughs, relaxing as the strangeness of their meeting subsides.

The landscape is completely unfamiliar to a city girl like Sharon. Harry talks about the climate and the people. Then he tells her stories about the pioneer days in Idaho. By the time they reach Ontario they are chatting like long-lost friends. "I thought about taking you out to dinner here in Ontario tonight, but then I thought it would be more fun to grill steaks while you and Josie get to know each other."

They arrive at the house. Harry shows Sharon her room and introduces Josie. He settles the two women on the deck with large glasses of a very good red wine.

"Perfect," Sharon sighs. "It's really peaceful here, isn't it?"

"Absolutely. Not much happens, but we do have beautiful sunsets." Harry picks up his glass and takes a long drink.

Josie laughs and raises her glass in a mock toast. "Here's to the happy couple."

Sharon blushes and takes a drink. Her head buzzes in a pleasant way. *I could get used to this.*

Harry refuses her help with dinner, so she sits with Josie and they have a second glass of wine and talk while Harry tosses a salad and puts the steaks on the grill. Sharon says, "I thought you might be a vegetarian."

Harry pulls a face, "No, I try to eat a healthy diet. We eat a lot of fish, and I like to garden so the vegetables are fresh. But, now and then, a good piece of red meat is just what the doctor ordered."

Dinner is served on the deck as the sunset lingers in the sky. "I guess I expected it to be colder," Sharon admits.

"It can be, and in the winter it's very cold," Josie says. "We've had a warm spring this year." She pushes her wheelchair back from the table. "I think I'm ready to call it a night. It's been lovely meeting you, Sharon. I look forward to tomorrow."

"Thank you for having me," Sharon realizes she sounds like her mother. Harry stands and follows Jose into the house.

The minutes seem to stretch out and Sharon begins to stack the dishes. She carries the plates into the kitchen. It's immaculate. Harry returns and she asks, "How do you keep it so clean when you cook? I make a mess just burning toast."

"It's a habit," Harry admits. "I like things tidy. Let me get these into the dishwasher, and then we can have another glass of wine."

They listen to music and talk about this and that and explore what they have in common and what is different. They laugh easily together. Sharon is glad she took the chance and came for the visit. She really could get used to this life. At eleven, Harry yawns and suggests that they head for bed. He walks her to her room, kisses her cheek, and says goodnight. Sharon falls asleep with a smile on her lips.

She wakes to the sound of voices and follows them to the kitchen. Harry and Josie are eating breakfast.

"Good morning, sleepyhead." Harry grins at her.

"You should have knocked on my door." Sharon is a little embarrassed to be standing in a strange kitchen wearing pajamas and a robe.

"We get up early, but that's doesn't mean you need to," Josie says. "You're on vacation. Harry, pour the girl a cup of coffee." Sharon sinks into a chair and gratefully sips on the coffee. It's very good coffee. She feels more comfortable at once.

"I thought we'd go for a hike today. I'm making a picnic. Do you like pickles in your tuna salad?" Harry asks.

"I do," Sharon admits. "Are you using your famous canned tuna?"

"Yep. You're going to love it."

Everything seems so easy and friendly here. It feels like she's known these two forever. Sharon wonders if this might be what falling in love is all about.

They set out on their hike straight from the back of the house. It takes only a few hundred feet before the house is hidden from view and they are walking through timberland. The air is clean and smells wonderful Sharon takes a deep breath. Harry smiles at her and takes her hand.

They emerge from the trees and find themselves at the side of beautiful lake. Mountains rise in the distance. Birds are singing and a butterfly floats by. Sharon laughs aloud. "Oh, Harry," she says, "it's so beautiful."

"And so are you," he says. He takes her in his arms and for the first time they kiss deeply and passionately. They smile at each other and kiss again. When they break apart Harry asks, "Are you hungry?"

Sharon grins. "I really am," she says. "I could eat an elephant." They take a blanket from Harry's backpack and spread out the food. Harry looks at the sandwiches and hands her one. "This is yours," he says, "with pickles for you and without pickles for me."

Sharon takes a big bite. "It's delicious. Maybe the best tuna salad I've ever had."

"Only maybe?" Harry teases.

Sharon takes another bite. "Absolutely the best." Harry smiles and watches her eat the sandwich. They stay by the lake for a while, skipping rocks and still talking. Sharon has never had so much fun on a date before. She wonders if she should tell Harry or if she should wait a bit; she decides to wait. He looks at his watch and says, "We need to get back. Josie will need her meds soon."

They walk back toward the house by a different route, and Sharon is surprised how close they were to his house all this time. He teases her about not being much use in the woods. Sharon stumbles and he catches her. "Are you okay?"

She nods but actually she doesn't feel too well. "I think I need a nap."

Harry holds her hand until they reach the house. "Come on," he says. "I'll tuck you in."

The room spins. Sharon's head aches. She closes her eyes and dozes off. When she wakes, the room is dark, and her head is still pounding. She sits up and everything tilts. She throws up and Harry opens the door. Her mouth is too dry to talk. Her heart is racing and she begins to shake violently. Harry sits beside her and strokes her hair. He tells her she is pretty. She tries to push him away, but the room tilts again and she falls back. Josie is standing at the door, watching. Sharon reaches out asking wordlessly for help. Harry continues to stoke her hair. Her head is going to explode she wishes she'd never gone online. The room goes black and Sharon's head rolls to the side.

Josie smiles sadly at Harry. "I thought we agreed that you wouldn't date anyone else," she says.

Harry shrugs. "I know," he says, "but we had that extra jar of bad tuna, and it seemed a shame to let it go to waste. Your idea about adding pickles to disguise the taste worked well. She loved her sandwich. I'm just going to clean up this mess and then let's have a nice cup of tea."

AUTHORS' BIOGRAPHIES:

April Baldrich is a lifelong lover of stories and adventure. Whether wandering the streets of Tokyo or the aisles of her local grocery store, there is a tale to be told. After moving from Delaware cross-country with a backpack and a dream, she has been a waitress, grocery clerk, biologist, respiratory therapist, and accounting clerk. She resides in Southern California with her husband and two cats.

Cornelia Feye is the founder of Konstellation Press, an independent publishing company producing fiction and poetry books as well as interdisciplinary events at the intersection of art, music, and literature. Her first novel, *Spring of Tears*, an art mystery set in France in 2011 won the San Diego Book Award for the mystery category. Her second mystery *House of the Fox* is set in the Anza-Borrego Desert and San Diego. Her third novel, *Private Universe,* a coming-of-age story and art mystery, was released in 2017. Publications include art historical essays and reviews in English and German. She received her M.A. in art history and anthropology from the University of Tübingen, Germany. After five years in New York, she moved to San Diego, where she taught Eastern and Western Art History. Her museum experience includes the Mingei International, The San Diego Museum of Art, the San Diego Museum of Man, and the California Center for the Arts, Escondido. From 2007 to 2017 she was the School of the Arts and Arts Education Director at the Athenaeum Music & Arts Library in La Jolla. In the 1970s she traveled around the world for seven years, and her adventures on the road have found their way into her writing. When she is not writing or teaching, she enjoys Rollerblading and dancing tango. www.konstellationpress.com

Max Feye, a San Diego native, is a student at the University of Southern California's School of Cinematic Arts, where he focuses on writing for screen and television. He aims to transform his love for writing surreal poetry, short stories, and scripts into new forms on the big screen. When he's not undertaking daunting tasks like that, he enjoys California burritos, collecting Hawaiian shirts, film photography, and creating digital art.

Tamara Merrill is a left brain/right brain woman. Her skills extend from writing fiction to writing computer programs, and to tackling any DIY project. Tamara admits to reading excessively (she has what she calls "a book-a-day habit"). Tamara published her first short story at the age of nine in the official Girl Scout magazine, *American Girl*. She continues to love the short story format and reads and writes them often. Tamara is the author of the popular Augustus Family Trilogy: *Family Lies*, *Family Matters*, and *Family Myths*. She has published multiple short stories in popular women's magazines and in anthologies. In addition to reading, Tamara often teaches in the adult education system and enjoys walking on the beach, crafts, painting, dining with friends, and travel. She is available to speak at book clubs—in person or via Skype. Tamara currently resides in Coronado, California. You can contact her through email, at Tamara@TamaraMerrill.com; Facebook, at @TamaraMerrillAuthor; or her website, TamaraMerrill.com.

Kate Porter's novel, *Lessons in Disguise* (Konstellation Press, 2017), follows the journey of an old book through 150 years of American history as the volume touches the lives of its eight owners. While working on a collection of poetry, Kate is also completing her next novel, *The Vagrant Darter*, a humorous and scandal-filled romp told in three voices—a naive husband, a deceitful wife, and a remarkably insightful fly-on-the-wall. Her prose and poetry have appeared in

Yankee Magazine and four anthologies. She began writing pieces for publication while in junior high and later wrote profile articles for *The Villager*, a monthly magazine in Rhode Island, where she lived with her husband and their daughter. Now residing in San Diego, Kate works as an editor and certified copyeditor, and she is a survivor of MS and chronic neurologic Lyme disease. She meets with readers at book events, book clubs, and libraries, where questions and lively discussions are encouraged. Please visit her website and blog, TheBookJourneys.com, or contact her at kaporterbooks@gmail.com.

Claire Rann has been reading, telling, and writing stories for as long as she can remember. After completing her BA in English and History at Amherst College, Claire earned her MA in Iranian History at St. Andrews in Scotland. She worked with Iraqi refugees resettled in Chicago for a year before moving to New York City to teach high school ESL and Special Education. A Chicagoland native whose twenties kept taking her to progressively colder places, Claire was very ready to relocate to San Diego in 2016. By day, she's a behavioral therapist helping kids with autism navigate our crazy world. By early morning and night, she writes to help herself (and, hopefully, her readers) understand that same crazy world. Claire mostly writes strange little fiction stories, including *Aim*, selected by judge Ann Beattie as the second-place winner in the 2016 WriterHouse fiction contest.

ALSO BY KONSTELLATION PRESS:

WWW.KONSTELLATIONPRESS.COM,
FACEBOOK@KONSTELLATIONPRESS

Spring of Tears, Cornelia Feye

Family Myths, Tamara Merrill

Lessons in Disguise, Kate Porter

Private Universe, Cornelia Feye

the wine tasted sweeter in the paper cups, carlos carrio

a tender force, melissa joseph

Captured Moments, Mary Kay Gardner

Crown City by the Sea, Jennifer M. Franks

barefoot monks with sullied toes, carlos carrio

A Mouthful of Murder, Andrea Carter

Crossing Paths, Susan Lewallen

CPSIA information can be obtained
at www.ICGtesting.com
Printed in the USA
FSHW010024300719
60518FS